LOV
INVIN

CW00919673

Barbara Cartland

Barbara Cartland Ebooks Ltd

This edition © 2018

ISBNs

9781788670975   EPUB

9781788670982   PAPERBACK

Book design by M-Y Books
m-ybooks.co.uk

THE BARBARA CARTLAND ETERNAL COLLECTION

The Barbara Cartland Eternal Collection is the unique opportunity to collect all five hundred of the timeless beautiful romantic novels written by the world's most celebrated and enduring romantic author.

Named the Eternal Collection because Barbara's inspiring stories of pure love, just the same as love itself, the books will be published on the internet at the rate of four titles per month until all five hundred are available.

The Eternal Collection, classic pure romance available worldwide for all time .

THE LATE DAME BARBARA CARTLAND

Barbara Cartland, who sadly died in May 2000 at the grand age of ninety eight, remains one of the world's most famous romantic novelists. With worldwide sales of over one billion, her outstanding 723 books have been translated into thirty six different languages, to be enjoyed by readers of romance globally.

Writing her first book 'Jigsaw' at the age of 21, Barbara became an immediate bestseller. Building upon this initial success, she wrote continuously throughout her life, producing bestsellers for an astonishing 76 years. In addition to Barbara Cartland's legion of fans in the UK and across Europe, her books have always been immensely popular in the USA. In 1976 she achieved the unprecedented feat of having books at numbers 1 & 2 in the prestigious B. Dalton Bookseller bestsellers list.

Although she is often referred to as the 'Queen of Romance', Barbara Cartland also wrote several historical biographies, six autobiographies and numerous theatrical plays as well as books on life, love, health and cookery. Becoming one of Britain's most popular media personalities and dressed in her trademark pink, Barbara spoke on radio and television about social and political issues, as well as making many public appearances.

In 1991 she became a Dame of the Order of the British Empire for her contribution to literature and her work for humanitarian and charitable causes.

Known for her glamour, style, and vitality Barbara Cartland became a legend in her own lifetime. Best remembered for her wonderful romantic novels and loved by millions of readers worldwide, her books remain treasured for their heroic heroes, plucky heroines and traditional values. But above all, it was Barbara Cartland's overriding belief in the positive power of love to help, heal and improve the quality of life for everyone that made her truly unique.

AUTHOR'S NOTE

Much of Victorian Imperial history depended on the fear of Russian intentions in India.

The most vulnerable frontier point of all lay in the North-West corner in the tangled country around Afghanistan, which was Alexander the Great's gateway to India.

Afghanistan was a very unreliable neighbour and the frontier area was inhabited by lawless Muslim tribes owing no definite allegiance to anybody and making it very difficult to establish and maintain a firm line of defence.

This was why *The Great Game* came into being, and the excitement, risk and secrecy about it was something that every intelligent and ambitious Englishman longed to be involved in.

The British pulled the Russians inexorably East and South, absorbing one after another the Khanates of Central Asia and preparing for the encirclement of India.

They were already building a railway across Siberia to the Far East and it was rumoured, although no one could actually confirm it, that they were building a railway in Turkestan, and planning the annexation of Tibet.

Queen Victoria was considerably disturbed about this and was continually asking questions of the Viceroy.

The British were posting their troops as close to the Russians as possible, although sometimes they thought that the actual possession of Afghanistan would become necessary.

The legend of the British arms in India, written about so brilliantly by Rudyard Kipling, was born out of the rocks and wadis of the North-West, where savage tribesmen lay in ambush behind the next rock.

The Afghans brooded behind the tribes and behind them all stood the Russians.

CHAPTER ONE
1887

Riding very fast Lucille put her horse at a high fence and leapt over it in style.

Patting the horse's neck, she exclaimed,

"That's a good boy! I am very pleased with you."

She pulled him in gradually.

As she did so, a man on a large stallion came from beneath the shelter of some trees where he had been watching her.

He then swept his tall hat from his head and she saw that he was exceedingly good-looking and very elegantly dressed.

She recognised that at last she was meeting the Marquis of Shawforde.

"May I congratulate you on the way you took that fence," he said. "I was just about to put my own horse at it, but I feel he would not do as well as yours."

Lucille smiled at him and he saw that she had two dimples, one on each side of her mouth.

She was in fact one of the prettiest girls he had ever seen.

Her fair hair was the colour of sunshine and her eyes as translucent as a mountain stream, she was just fantastic.

He thought that she must be a visitor to this part of the country.

There was a silence between them for a moment.

And then Lucille said,

"I am waiting to watch your Lordship's performance."

The Marquis raised his eyebrows.

"If you know who I am," he replied, "I can only ask you to be kind enough to introduce yourself."

"My name is Lucille Winterton."

He wrinkled his brow as he concentrated before he responded,

"I have not seen you in London for, if I had, I should not have forgotten you."

"You have not seen me in London," Lucille replied, "for the simple reason that I have not yet been there!"

"You live *here*?" he asked incredulously.

"I live just outside the village and not far from your Lordship's main gate."

"Then I shall not lose you again."

She laughed as if she thought it somewhat presumptuous of him.

Drawing his horse nearer to hers, he then said,

"I must suppose that, as you are riding on my ground, it is something you ought not to do."

"It may be your ground technically," Lucille replied, "but for years, if not centuries, it has been the local Racecourse. Everybody in the village and many people in the County as well race and jump their horses here."

She gave him a quick glance and added,

"If you forbid us to do so, I think there will be a revolution!"

The Marquis laughed.

"I promise you I shall not do that, especially as I have met *you* here this morning."

He accentuated the word 'you'.

Lucille's eyes were twinkling as she replied,

"If you only knew how envied I shall be by everybody in the vicinity."

"Why?" the Marquis enquired.

"Because they have all been looking forward to meeting you and were very disappointed that when you gave exciting parties at The Hall they were not invited."

The Marquis laughed.

"Is that what they were expecting?"

"Of course they were, my Lord," Lucille said. "They thought when you inherited that things would change at the Big House, only to find that, where your neighbours are concerned, it is exactly the same as it was before."

"That is certainly something that shall be remedied," the Marquis declared. "When will you dine with me?"

"Now you are making me embarrassed, my Lord. It sounds as if I was fishing for an invitation."

"I promise you will be invited, whether you were fishing or not." the Marquis retorted.

He looked at her intently, as if to make sure she was real, and added,

"Are you telling me that there are more beautiful young women like yourself living at my gates? It is something I can hardly believe."

Lucille laughed and replied,

"You will have to find out for yourself. All I am waiting to do now is to gallop home and cry, 'I have met him! I have met him!'"

"Now you are making me feel as if I have behaved badly," the Marquis complained.

"Which, of course, you have!" Lucille answered.

He looked at her in surprise before he laughed again.

He was thinking as he did so that this young woman was prettier than anyone he had seen in London or anywhere else.

She was also very different from the gauche girls he always avoided at the balls he attended.

He had always understood that they were shy and tongue-tied.

"Are you going to answer my question?" he asked aloud. "I invited you to dinner."

Lucille looked away from him.

"I very much doubt that I shall be allowed to accept."

"Who will prevent you from doing so?"

"My sister and if Papa was alive, I am sure he would have made me refuse."

"Why? Why?" the Marquis enquired.

"Because Papa felt that your father was behaving badly to some of the poorer people in the village and my sister considers your parties an insult!"

"An insult?" the Marquis exclaimed in surprise. "What does she know about them?"

Lucille laughed.

"Surely you are aware, my Lord, that everything you do at Shaw Hall is known in the village, almost before it happens and is repeated and re-repeated around the County as if on the wind."

"I had no idea of that."

"Well, we had nothing much to talk about until you arrived," Lucille said frankly, "and I am quite certain that what we have heard has lost nothing in the telling."

She was thinking that the footmen, whose number had increased since the Marquis had inherited last year, all came from the village.

They regaled their families, as all the young housemaids did, with stories of the Marquis's behaviour and they kept everyone from the Vicar downwards in an almost permanent state of shock.

The last Marquis had died after a long and lingering illness and this meant that his huge house had always seemed to be enveloped in gloom.

Everybody had attended his funeral in the village Church that stood in a corner of the Park and was where a large number of the family were buried.

It had been like the end of an era.

"Things will be better now," the locals maintained optimistically.

But they were not prepared for the impact that the young Marquis made.

Two months later he had held his first party and filled the house with his London friends.

Generous-minded people said it was not surprising that he should want to enjoy the company of beautiful women and to dance in the ballroom, which had not been opened for many years.

Who could expect him to sit as his father had during his long illness, refusing to see visitors and just waiting to die?

"But a party be one thing, an orgy another!" Mrs. Geary who kept the grocer shop said tartly.

Everybody who listened agreed with her. There were stories that the gentlemen drank too much and that ladies with painted faces and crimson lips took part in 'high jinks'.

They slid down the banisters and danced, when it was a moonlit night, on the roof.

They wore, it was said in a shocked whisper, their nightgowns!

Games were introduced like 'Hunting the Fox' through the huge State Rooms after dinner with the gentlemen blowing hunting horns.

The 'fox,' or rather the 'foxes in question, were the women.

They hid themselves in strange places and then 'belonged' to whoever captured them.

What happened then was considered too outrageous for any of the young women's ears.

Certainly not for the daughters of the Squire, as Colonel Robert Winterton had always been called.

His estate was a small one compared to that of his neighbour, the Marquis.

But The Manor House of Little Bunbury had been known as the Squire's house, even before the Wintertons inhabited it. They had now lived there for over a hundred years.

The advent of the young Marquis, fifth in the line of succession, had definitely cheered up Little Bunbury.

Yet so far no one had met him personally and everything that was known about him was hearsay.

He had not spent his childhood at Shaw Hall as might have been expected.

His father and mother had separated when he was quite a small boy, but there had been nothing so vulgar as a divorce.

But the Marchioness had taken her son to live with her parents in the North of England.

And the Marquis had stayed, when he was at home, alone at The Hall.

When he was younger, this was not very frequent. He was in the Diplomatic Service and had no intention of retiring when he inherited his father's title.

Instead he went from Embassy to Embassy, preferring those in the Far East to any other part of the world.

He only returned very briefly at long intervals to the family mansion and it had therefore housed only two old aunts who were unmarried.

They gradually grew too old to take part in any kind of entertainment and the house became like a morgue.

The local people, therefore, had high hopes that things would change when the new Marquis arrived.

There were naturally, a great number of rumours circulating about him.

He was exceedingly handsome, enjoyed the nightlife of London and was a good rider to hounds.

"We shall see him out hunting," Lucille had said excitedly to her sister.

She was to be disappointed.

When the hunting season came, it was learned that the young Marquis had opened his Hunting Lodge in Leicestershire.

He had joined the smartest pack of hounds in the County, which was the Quorn and there was no way that Little Bunbury in Hertfordshire could compete.

They could only wait hopefully, month after month.

When they had almost despaired of ever seeing their elusive landlord, the Marquis arrived.

It was then, the village realised, that he had discovered that Shaw Hall was within easy driving distance from London.

It was therefore an excellent place for him to enjoy a weekend.

The first party was awaited with excitement.

And there was also the hope that the Marquis would call on some of his tenants.

The farmers were looking forward to telling him about their crops and the shepherds about their flocks.

The grooms, who were all growing old, were hoping that the stables would now be filled with well-bred horses.

The grooms' one wish did come true.

Lucille had listened with delight to the description of horses that had Arab blood in them and they had each cost an astronomical sum.

Although she had not told her sister, Delia, what she intended to do, she had ridden to the stables as soon as the Marquis had returned to London.

She coaxed Hanson, the Head Groom, who had been at The Hall for over forty years, to show her his new tenants.

"They are absolutely marvellous, Delia," she had exclaimed. "You have never seen better horses!"

Her sister had given her a long lecture on going to The Hall uninvited and Lucille had therefore not told her what she was doing on her subsequent visits.

Now, seeing the Marquis mounted on one of the horses that she had most admired, she suggested,

"Shall I race you? If we start at the end of the field, we can take three jumps and then circle back to the starting place by going behind that clump of rhododendrons."

She pointed out the way and the Marquis asked,

"What is the prize?"

"A ride on one of your horses," Lucille replied.

"I can think of something more exciting than that," the Marquis answered, "and I will tell you when I have won."

"Never count your chickens!" Lucille warned him.

They took their places at what she told him was the traditional starting place.

It was an exciting ride.

Lucille knew, as she took the last fence half a length behind the Marquis, that she had never enjoyed herself so much.

It was by a superb feat of riding on her part that she was only just behind the Marquis at the Winning Post.

They were both laughing as they pulled in their horses.

It had been a wild gallop to the finish.

"You ride better than any woman I have ever seen!" the Marquis exclaimed.

"Thank you," Lucille answered a little breathlessly, "but actually my sister is a better rider than I am."

"If you also tell me she is more beautiful than you, I shall not believe you," was the reply.

"Well, she is. And perhaps one day you will condescend to meet her."

"Are you telling me that I should have called on you before now?"

Lucille laughed.

"It is what a great number of people living near you expected."

"Now we are back where we started," the Marquis said, "but I shall enjoy it, now I have met you."

"Perhaps I should point out, my Lord," Lucille countered primly, "that we have not been formally introduced."

"It's too late for that," the Marquis answered, "but I won the race and you owe me a prize. I will tell you what that is tonight when you dine with me."

"Are you really having another party?"

"Actually," the Marquis said, "I had intended returning to London, but if you will dine with me, nothing will drag me away!"

Lucille opened her eyes very wide.

"Are you really – suggesting that we should – dine alone?"

"Of course I am. There are a great many things I want to say to you which would be impossible with a crowd of people listening."

Lucille laughed.

"I would like to thank your Lordship for your kind invitation, but regret that unfortunately I have another engagement."

"What do you mean by that?" the Marquis enquired.

"If you want the truth, I would never, under any circumstances, be allowed to dine alone with the notorious, raffish and much talked about Marquis of Shawforde!"

"I have never heard such nonsense," the Marquis said, "and I want to see you!"

Lucille did not answer and, after a moment, riding beside her, he said,

"You are not seriously telling me that I cannot entertain you tonight?"

Lucille looked at him from under her eyelashes.

They were unexpectedly dark compared to her hair.

"I assure you that you will find, after what we have heard about you, Mamas will hustle their daughters away when you appear and husbands will lock up their wives."

The Marquis threw back his head and laughed.

"Is it really as bad as that?"

"Rather worse," Lucille answered frankly.

He pulled in his horse.

Without really thinking about it, she did the same.

"Then what are we going to do?" he asked. "You know, Lucille, I want to see you again."

Just for a moment their eyes met.

And it was impossible for either of them to look away.

Then Lucille said,

"I think that is up to you. Goodbye, my Lord, and thank you."

Before the Marquis could realise what she was doing, she had touched her horse with her whip.

Then she was galloping away from him.

She wove in and out of the trees with an expertise that told him she was familiar with the almost invisible path.

It took Lucille to an entrance at the end of the village.

It was the nearest way to the 'Racecourse' where they had been riding.

The Marquis did not follow her.

He merely watched her until she was out of sight.

Then he rode slowly back through the Park towards his house.

*

Lucille reached The Manor and rode directly into the stables.

A groom hurried to take her horse from her.

"'Ad a nice ride, Miss Lucille?" he enquired.

"Delightful!" Lucille answered. "And Dragonfly flew over the fences. I shall definitely ride him in the next steeplechase."

"You do that, Miss Lucille, and I'll back you!" the groom answered.

Lucille smiled at him and ran to the house.

It was a very beautiful old Manor, built originally in Tudor times. It had been added to and improved by generation who had inhabited it since.

Lucille's mother had redecorated it from top to toe when her husband had brought her here on their marriage and it had been very little changed over the ensuing years.

Lucille ran into the large drawing room on the ground floor, which was where they always sat. It overlooked the rose garden with its sundial in the centre of it.

Her sister, Delia, was arranging the first buds from their mother's favourite rose tree in a vase under the window.

She looked up as Lucille entered.

Anyone seeing them together would have realised that there was a striking likeness between the two sisters.

The exception was that their characters and personalities were so different.

It showed in their eyes and, to anyone who was perceptive, in the aura that they were surrounded by.

Delia was also fair, but her eyes were grey, the soft grey of a pigeon's breast.

There was something ethereal about her, which made her seem reserved beside the glowing exuberance of Lucille and yet at the same time spiritual.

She was beautiful.

Anyone who looked at her had to look and look again.

Lucille's loveliness was as obvious as the sunshine and as brilliant as a cloudless sky.

"Delia! Delia. What do you think?" she cried as she entered the room. "I have met the Marquis!"

Delia stiffened, holding a half-opened white rose in her hand.

"The Marquis?" she repeated. "Where did you meet him?"

"On the Racecourse, and he is extraordinarily handsome, and absolutely charming."

"Did you talk to him?"

"Of course I talked to him," Lucille replied, "and I raced him over the jumps. He was riding the most magnificent horse you can imagine. So, of course, he won."

"I suppose I should have warned you not to go riding on the Racecourse when the Marquis was at home," Delia pointed out slowly.

"There is nowhere else to ride around here, as you well know and anyway we were bound to meet him sooner or later. I told him he should have called on us."

"Lucille, you did not do anything of the sort!"

"Yes, I did and he asked me to dinner."

Delia gave a little cry of horror before she asserted,

"Listen, Lucille, I have not said this before because there was no point, as it seemed unlikely we should ever meet the Marquis. But now that you have talked to him it is something you must not do again."

"Why not?" Lucille asked.

"You know the answer to that as well as I do," Delia replied. "He has caused a scandal by his behaviour and everybody in the County is shocked at what we have heard about his riotous parties."

"You have never been to one of them," Lucille answered, "so how can you be sure that what has been repeated in the village is not just a lot of lies?"

"I am perfectly prepared to believe that some of it has been exaggerated and invented," Delia admitted. "At the same time people who have met him in London have been horrified by the way he has been behaving."

"Well, personally, I found him absolutely delightful!" Lucille parried defiantly.

"I think, dearest, you are hardly capable of judging a man of that sort."

"I want to dine with him."

"That is impossible!" Delia objected. "Completely and absolutely impossible! You know that Papa would be horrified that he has behaved so badly towards the people on his estate."

"Perhaps I could persuade him to behave better?"

Delia laughed and it was a very pretty sound.

"Now you are imagining yourself to be one of the heroines in those ridiculous novelettes you read!"

"Why not?" Lucille enquired.

"Because they always 'reform the rake' so that he becomes overnight a good well-behaved man who will never sin again. You know that does not happen in real life."

"I am sure it does," Lucille argued, "but we don't hear about it."

"I am afraid history proves you wrong," Delia said. "Anyway the answer is definitely 'no'."

"Now you are being unfair and horrid to me!" Lucille protested. "I would love to go to dinner at The Hall, if only to see what changes the Marquis has made since he has been there."

"And have the whole village and everybody in the County throwing up their hands in horror?" Delia asked.

Lucille did not reply, and she went on,

"You are coming out this year and it is very important, dearest, that you should make a good impression."

Her voice was very serious as she went on,

"I cannot imagine that if you acquire a bad reputation you will be asked to the balls and parties by the mothers of other girls of your age."

As she spoke, Delia knew by the expression on her young sister's face that she was aware that she was speaking the truth.

She put down the vase and, crossing the room, she sat down beside Lucille.

"Listen, dearest," she said, "I know it is frustrating for you, because we are still in mourning for Papa, that you cannot be presented at Court this spring."

She put her hand on Lucille's arm and continued,

"But your Godmother has definitely promised that she will give a ball for you in October and then you will be able to accept all the many invitations that I am quite certain you will receive."

"In the meantime," Lucille said in a sulky voice, "I have to talk to the cabbages!"

"Surely you can do slightly better than cabbages?" Delia protested. "And I intended to talk to you about giving a few dinner parties."

"Can I invite the Marquis?"

"No!"

"Why not? After all, he is living next door."

Delia rose to her feet.

She walked, although she was not aware of it, with an exquisite grace towards the mantelpiece.

"You know I dislike listening to gossip," she said, "but it is impossible to stop Flo or any of the housemaids talking."

Lucille knew this to be true.

Flo, who came from the village every day, always arrived with the latest gossip and, as Delia had just said, nothing would stop her talking.

"Flo said," Delia went on, "that not only has the Marquis become very much involved with Lady Swinneton, who is a famous beauty, but there is also a rumour, although, of course, one cannot believe all one hears, that he is engaged to be married."

She did not look round, but she was aware that Lucille had stiffened.

"Engaged to be married?" she queried.

"I was not really listening, but it was to somebody very important – I think a Duke's daughter."

There was silence and then Lucille said in a small voice,

"What you are really saying is that he is not likely to be interested in a local girl from his village."

"I think perhaps anybody would be interested in you, dearest," Delia replied. "You are very very pretty and very amusing, but you know that the Marquis would never consider you for a wife."

"And why not?" Lucille asked bluntly.

"Because, dearest, blue blood, where aristocrats are concerned, is matched with blue blood and their marriages are arranged rather like Royalty."

"So to marry a Marquis, I have to be the daughter of one or my father should be a Duke!"

"Exactly," Delia said, "and usually the bride contributes something valuable to the marriage."

"What is that?"

"The Marquis's mother was very rich as well as an heiress in her own right. But, as you know, that did not make the marriage a happy one."

"What was wrong with the last Marquis's marriage that she left him?" Lucille asked her sister.

"I honestly don't know, except that Papa said he was a disagreeable obstinate man and, as you are aware, he and Papa did not speak towards the end of his life."

Lucille made a sound of exasperation.

"It does seem to me extraordinary. I am sitting here with nothing to do and nobody to talk to. When I do meet a handsome charming man, I am told that I am to have nothing to do with him!"

"I am sorry, dearest," Delia said, "it is only because I love you and want you to be such a success when you make your debut that I do *not* want anything or anyone like the Marquis to spoil it."

Lucille rose from the chair that she had thrown herself into.

"I do understand, Delia. I do, really. And I know you are thinking of me. But you must admit we are short of young men in this part of the world at present."

She went on in a sarcastic voice,

"They are either the same age as I am, brainless and chinless, or alternatively they are as old as Methuselah!"

Delia laughed.

"Everything will change when you go to London and please, please, dearest, do be sensible. You know as well as I do that an introduction by the Marquis of Shawforde would not be accepted in the best circles."

Lucille giggled as if she could not help it.

"As I have a suspicion that the 'best circles' are going to be pompous, critical and very very dull, I feel like risking the Marquis and enjoying myself."

"Oh, Lucille, please!" Delia urged her.

But already her sister had gone out of the room and she could hear her footsteps crossing the hall.

She gave a little sigh and finished the flowers in the window.

She was thinking as she did so that the sooner their cousin arrived to chaperone them, the better. She had thought when her father died that there would be no need for an older woman in the house.

Yet now that Lucille was back from school, she was afraid that people would think it strange that two young women were living alone at the Manor.

For the last two years of his life Delia had looked after her father devotedly, but it meant that she had not been a *debutante* in any sense of the word.

There had been no special parties or balls given for her.

Soon she would be twenty-one and she thought that she was old enough to look after her impetuous younger sister without any assistance.

Now she was not so sure.

She was well aware that Lucille was so lovely that she would attract any man the instant he saw her.

She also knew that being at a Finishing School in France had swept away her shyness. It had actually given her a poise and a polish that was not usually found amongst young English girls.

'She will be a huge success in London,' she reflected confidently.

It never occurred to her that she herself should enter the Social world, she had given that up so that she could look after her father.

Now she was worrying as to how she could prevent Lucille from throwing away her chances of being a social success.

She would certainly do so if she consorted with a man who was condemned for his suspect behaviour not only in Little Bunbury but also in London.

Delia would not have been so sure of this if she had not received a letter from one of their cousins.

She had promised to keep an eye on Lucille when she eventually appeared in London under her Godmother's wing.

She had written to her telling her what was arranged.

And she had received a reply, which read,

"Of course I will do what I can for Lucille, but she could not do better than to be staying with Lady Morgan, whom everybody admires and who gives marvellous parties.

I have been invited to only one of them, but I shall never forget how distinguished all the guests were and I met the most fascinating Spanish Prince, who I will tell you about some other time.

I learnt, however, that heh as rather a naughty reputation and, talking of that I must tell you that your neighbour, the Marquis of Shawforde, has succeeded in shocking everybody in the whole Social world!

They say that all the grand hostesses are considering striking him off their guest lists, but, of course, that will not worry the very fast set that he moves in.

There has been a great deal of talk about him and Lady Swinneton, who is so lovely that people stand on the chairs in Rotten Row just to see her pass by.

There is a rumour that Lord Swinneton is thinking of calling the Marquis out, even though, as you know, duelling is now strictly forbidden.

But Lady Swinneton is not the only one! His Lordship is supposed to have climbed in through the bedroom window of a very beautiful and influential lady, only to find that she was not alone!

I will tell you all about it when we next meet. Until then tell Lucille that I will find some charming young gentlemen to partner her.

I send you both my love. "

Delia sighed when she read the letter.

It was first a sigh of relief and it was a joy to know that there would be a number of people to help Lucille when she first appeared in London.

But it was also a sigh of regret that their next-door neighbour should behave so badly.

There were so many things that needed doing in the village and the old Marquis had been difficult and disagreeable about spending money.

She had hoped when he died that his son would make up for his deficiencies.

Instead, it was quite obvious that the new Marquis was not in the least interested either in his estate or in the people who had served his family for generations.

Living always in the country, Delia was aware that country folk needed encouragement and they wanted somebody to care about what they were doing and how they were faring.

It was her father who had explained to her that farming was a precarious life.

No one could be sure if the weather would not ruin the crops. There could be a fall of snow in the spring when the ewes were lambing.

A drought could be disastrous and too much rain could leave everything sodden.

There were many problems and difficulties and even the most skilful farmer appreciated it when his landlord stood behind him in troubled times.

'How can anyone explain all this to a tiresome young man,' she asked herself, 'who wants only to enjoy himself in an outrageous fashion?'

She told herself firmly that it was Lucille she must look after.

How could she have imagined for one moment that the Marquis would interfere in their quiet uneventful lives?

'If he continues to stay here, I shall have to take Lucille away,' she decided.

Then she was quite sure that she was making a mountain out of a molehill.

The Marquis's house party had all left, as Flo had told the household when she came in for work this morning.

It was therefore extremely unlikely that, Lucille or no Lucille, he would stay on at the Hall alone.

That he had invited her to dinner seemed strange.

Certainly not the behaviour of a gentlemen towards an innocent young girl.

Delia was frightened by her own thoughts as she pushed what was left of the roses into the vase.

Then leaving the drawing room she hurried up the stairs to find Lucille.

CHAPTER TWO

Lucille rode her horse slowly up the steep incline to the Folly. It stood on top of one of the hills overlooking the Shaw estate.

It had been built by the second Marquis, who had been known as an eccentric.

It boasted a tall thin tower rather like a lighthouse, but the bottom part, for no apparent purpose, had an Oriental look with trelliswork windows.

In the centre there was a statue of Krishna, the Indian God of Love.

It was a favourite place of generations of children who would play hide-and-seek" among the bushes that had grown up outside.

Then, climbing up the twisting stone stairs to the top, they had a panoramic view over the countryside.

In spite of Delia's warning, Lucille had met the Marquis again several times on the Racecourse.

The previous morning he had said,

"As you will not dine with me, I have an idea where we might have luncheon alone without anybody being aware of it."

"You will be clever if you can find any place where you will not find prying eyes," Lucille answered.

As she spoke, she looked over her shoulder apprehensively.

"I have thought of a place," the Marquis said triumphantly. "It's the Folly."

Lucille looked at him in surprise and then laughed.

"It is certainly an idea."

"I hear that my father caused great offence by closing it to the outside public and so, if you and I go there, it is doubtful if anyone will know about it."

"That is true," Lucille admitted, "but at the same time I ought to say 'no'."

She had already found it impossible to say 'no' to the Marquis.

He had pleaded that they meet very early in the morning on the Racecourse and she had agreed.

"I have been told that you ride early," he persisted, "so nobody would be surprised at your doing anything so customary. Then, if I just 'happen' to be riding my own horse at the same time, it can hardly be a crime if we meet each other by 'accident'."

There was in fact nothing accidental about it, except that it was the first morning after Delia had made it quite clear to Lucille that she was not to see the Marquis again.

She had been firm and indeed very eloquent on the subject of the harm that he would do her.

Lucille had, however, after Delia had left her, sat thinking of how handsome the Marquis was and how amusing.

She had always found it irksome at school when the other pupils related the romantic incidents that had happened to them during the holiday.

There was, however, very little entertainment for teenagers in the vicinity of Little Bunbury and so Lucille had to remain silent.

Now she was almost sorry that she was not going back for another term so that she could describe the Marquis and it would make all her friends envious.

'I am determined to see him again,' she told herself in the darkness.

When she fell asleep, she was feeling rebellious.

*

Lucille awoke very early, far earlier than she usually did, and decided that it was impossible to stay in bed.

The sun was shining and the birds were singing loudly outside her window.

She wanted to ride Swallow, her favourite horse, and put him over the jumps.

'Just because Delia says I am not to meet the Marquis, I have no intention of ruining my chances of winning the steeplechase,' she told herself.

This was a local event that was attended by all the farmers in the neighbourhood, as well as their landlords. And in the Ladies' Race there were usually quite a number of experienced competitors.

This year Lucille was determined to be the winner.

She climbed out of bed and dressed herself quickly in a riding skirt and blouse as it would be too hot to wear a jacket.

Instead of a hat she plaited her long fair hair and pinned it closely to her head in a chignon.

Hardly looking at herself in the mirror, she hurried as silently as possible down the stairs.

She had no wish to waken her sister and if she did she would only be warned once again not to come in contact with the wicked Marquis.

"If you should meet him," Delia had said firmly, "be polite and then come back home immediately."

He was not likely to be riding at five o'clock in the morning, Lucille thought, but she could not resist an irrepressible hope that he would be.

She was not disappointed as he was already on the Racecourse waiting for her.

As she rode towards him, he swept off his hat.

She thought to herself that he was even more handsome than he had been the day before.

"I did not expect you to be here so early," she said as she reached his side.

"That is what I was sure you would be thinking," he replied.

They looked at each other and there was really no need for words.

Then he said simply,

"I had to see you!"

With an effort Lucille looked away from him.

"My sister has forbidden me to meet you again."

"That is what I expected, but you know we have to see each other."

"It is something I must not do!"

"Why should you say that?"

"Because Delia says you will ruin my reputation and I shall be asked to none of the balls when I come to London."

There was silence and then the Marquis said,

"Do you really want me to leave you?"

Lucille parted her lips to say that was what he must do.

Then as she looked into his eyes she was lost.

"Now, listen," he demanded, "I have no wish to hurt you and I swear I would not do so. But I have lain awake all night thinking about you and I have to go on seeing you."

Lucille would have replied, but he went on,

"I have to talk to you, to look at you and we have a great deal to discover about each other."

The way he spoke was so beguiling that all Lucille's good resolutions flew out of her head.

They raced round the course.

Because the Marquis won for the second time, they changed horses.

Then Lucille was the winner by, she admitted, only a nose, but she thought that it was the most exciting thing that had ever happened to her.

The Marquis took charge.

"If we are going to see each other without you getting into a row over it," he asserted, "I am now going to leave you."

Lucille repressed a little exclamation of dismay and he continued,

"But I have to see you again today. Where can we meet?"

"It's impossible!"

Then Lucille gave a little cry.

"I know that my sister is meeting the Vicar at three-thirty."

That was the beginning, and the next day they rode together at dawn and the next, confident that no one knew about it.

Again later in the afternoon whenever it was possible, they met in one of the thickest woods on the estate.

Now the Marquis had suggested they should have luncheon in the Folly and because it sounded so amusing Lucille could not refuse.

She told Delia that she was riding some distance to see a friend. It was a girl of her own age whose father was the High Sheriff of the County.

"That will be lovely for you, dearest," Delia said, "and persuade Eileen to come to dinner here next Wednesday and we will give a party."

"I will ask her," Lucille agreed.

"I think Timothy Bladen will be home," Delia said reflectively, "and we can ask him."

Lucille made a little grimace, but her sister did not notice.

She was making a list of such young men as there were in the neighbourhood and now she sat down to write letters of invitation to them.

Wearing her prettiest riding habit and a hat to make herself look more formal, Lucille left The Manor at eleven-thirty.

She rode away looking very elegant and extremely pretty.

Delia thought for the first time that perhaps her sister should be escorted by a groom.

The two men who looked after their horses were both getting on in years and anyway Lucille had always ridden alone ever since they were children.

It was not really a careless thing to do in the countryside where they knew everybody and where convenience invariably outweighed social protocol.

'I suppose really,' Delia said to herself, 'now that Lucille is grown up, I should engage a younger groom.'

It was just a passing thought.

She forgot about it as she hurried into the house.

There were innumerable small duties that had fallen onto her shoulders since her mother died.

*

Lucille did not hurry herself.

She knew that it would take her far less time to reach the Folly and she did not wish to be waiting for the Marquis.

'He,' she told herself, 'should be waiting for *me*!'

All the things the girls at school had said about attracting a man now came to her mind.

"The greatest mistake," one of the French pupils had said who was older than Lucille, "is to look as if you are running after a man rather than enticing him to run after you."

"How does one do that?" another girl enquired.

"It is called being evasive," the French girl replied. "My sister taught me that."

"I thought your sister was married," someone pointed out.

"She is," was the answer. "But it was, of course, arranged by my parents and, although she is very fond of her husband, she is not in love with him."

The girls listened fascinated, but it had been Lucille who had asked,

"Are you saying that your sister has young men running after her even though she has a husband?"

"Of course she has," the French girl replied. "Her house in Paris is filled with young men who write her poems, smuggle her love letters through her lady's maid and one of them even fought a duel because another man disparaged her!"

It all sounded wildly romantic, but Lucille had never thought that it could happen to her.

'I must make certain he does not think me fast or immoral, like the women Flo describes staying at The Hall,' she told herself.

It had been quite easy to obtain information from Flo about the parties the Marquis gave.

"I've never 'eard such goin's-on, Miss Lucille," Flo said, "but I'm not tellin' you about 'em!"

She then proceeded, of course, to relate everything that had happened in some detail.

Even allowing for Flo's imagination and what Lucille was sure was a certain amount of exaggeration, the parties definitely sounded rowdy.

They were certainly a complete contrast to the gloomy pomposity that had always existed at The Hall.

Because he was a young man she could understand the Marquis enjoying what the village thought was outrageous.

Yet, Lucille was intelligent enough not to wish to be classified in the same category as those guests, women who would dance in their nightgowns on the roof and slide down the banisters showing an exceedingly immodest amount of leg.

She had also, having lived in Paris, a much better idea than Delia had of what else happened at such parties.

She thought, although she was not sure, that the women in question were the English version of the French *courtesans.*

Although the girls at school were supposed to know nothing of such improper creatures, they continually talked about them.

They repeated what they had heard their brothers, their cousins, their uncles and even their fathers say.

They had sometimes found pictures of such women in magazines and newspapers and they smuggled them into the school to show their friends.

Lucille was therefore well aware that there was a dividing line between a lady and a *courtesan* that could never be bridged.

She was a little apprehensive after what Delia had said about the Marquis's engagement.

If she was not careful, he would not think of her as the lady she believed herself to be.

But it seemed impossible that he should think anything else.

After all she was her father's daughter and no one was more proud of his antecedents than Colonel Winterton.

She understood, however, that the Marquis of Shawforde was only a step below Royalty and he consequently considered anyone lower than himself to be of little consequence.

This was certainly the attitude of French aristocrats.

Lucille was well aware that half the pupils at the school near Paris where she had been educated had already had their husbands chosen for them.

Ancient lineage must not be impaired by an infusion of red blood, but it was something that she had accepted as peculiar to foreigners.

So in a way it was a shock to find the same thing existed in England.

She approached the Folly, knowing that she was playing truant and deceiving Delia, whom she loved.

At the same time she was determined that the Marquis should treat her with respect.

'We are not doing any harm,' she argued with herself as if to placate her conscience. 'It is simply that it is fun to be with an agreeable young man rather than having little or nothing to do until I can go to London.'

As she neared the Folly, she saw the Marquis's horse tethered to a tree nearby and she thought with a leap of her heart that he was there.

He must have been watching for her as she had come up the hill.

When she reached the summit, he stepped out from amongst the trees.

He then lifted her from the saddle.

Lucille could not help a little thrill run through her.

His hands seemed to linger on her waist rather longer than was necessary.

"You have come!" he exclaimed. "I was so afraid that something might prevent you."

"I had to lie and be deceitful to do so," Lucille answered, "which is, as you know, something I very much dislike."

"You look lovely," he said. "So lovely that I am convinced every time I see you that you are not real."

"I am real and very hungry!" Lucille smiled. "I have been wondering how you could have brought our luncheon here without anybody being aware of what you were doing."

"I was very clever," the Marquis said complacently. "I told my butler that I intended to explore the estate and had no idea where I would find anything to eat. 'Tell the chef to pack me something edible,' I said, 'and plenty of it in case I have to share what I have with me with a farmer or anyone else I am talking to at the time'."

Lucille laughed and he added,

"You might say it was rather clever of me. Go and see what is waiting for you!"

She went through the entrance of the Folly.

On the marble step of the plinth where Krishna was dancing was spread out their luncheon.

It was certainly sumptuous and very different from what she would have eaten at The Manor.

There was caviar, *pâté de foie gras*, chicken in aspic and a selection of cheeses and the chef obviously thought that all this was appropriate for a man.

There was also a bottle of champagne.

"A feast for the Gods," the Marquis declared.

It flashed through Lucille's mind that this was how she wanted him to think of her.

Then, because it was hot, she pulled off her jacket and her hat.

"What have you been doing since I last saw you?" she asked.

She was conscious as she spoke that his eyes were on her face.

In consequence she found it difficult to speak lightly.

"I have just been waiting until I could see you again," the Marquis replied.

"I am flattered, but I hope you listened to what I said to you yesterday."

"About getting to know the farmers and the people on the estate?" the Marquis enquired. "I called on one this morning."

"Did you really?" Lucille asked. "That is good."

"A nice man called Jackson. He told me all his troubles and I promised that I would do up some of his buildings and repair the roof of his farm."

Lucille clasped her hands together.

"That is wonderful. I know that everybody on the estate will be impressed and there are manyother things that need your attention."

She thought as she spoke that she had been very clever.

She had found out from Delia without her being aware of it what was vitally needed and it had been quite easy to make Delia talk.

Lucille had known that, if the Marquis was seeing to his farms and his estate, it would be a good excuse for him to stay in the country and away from London.

Flo had made it very clear that there was a great deal of speculation as to why he was content to be alone in the Big House.

"Seems strange as 'e's never been 'ere afore, Miss Lucille, that 'e should just be a-sittin' there by 'isself. Mrs.

Geary thinks 'e's probably bin crossed in love, but 'e could never 'ave married any of them creatures 'e 'ad to stay."

"Why not?" Lucille had asked with pretended innocence.

"'Cause they're not the sort of women your mother'd want you to know about," Flo had replied after a pause, "and, as for a man marryin' one of them, there's no necessity for that!"

Flo had spoken, as usual, without thinking. Then, as if she realised that she was being indiscreet, she returned to black-leading the fireplace.

Now Lucille sat down on the lower step of the Folly and said,

"I confess to being greedy. Can we begin?"

"I wish I could paint a picture of you," the Marquis ventured. "You did not tell me that it was very appropriate that we should meet here."

"Why appropriate?" Lucille enquired as she helped herself to caviar.

"Because it is a Temple to the God of Love!"

Lucille looked up at the dancing God, which had become a little damaged over the years.

It still personified the joy and youthfulness that the Indians associated him with.

"I think perhaps he is giving us his blessing," the Marquis suggested.

"I doubt it," Lucille replied in a practical voice. "He is far more likely to be shocked that I am behaving in an extremely reprehensible manner."

"Nonsense!" the Marquis parried.

"I was thinking last night that Delia is right," she continued. "If any of our neighbours knew that I was here, I should be ostracised."

"Why should anybody know?"

"Even the birds and the bees gossip in the country and, quite frankly, I am frightened."

"Are you trying to tell me that you don't wish to see me again?" the Marquis asked in a strange voice.

"Of course I want to see you," Lucille replied. "It would be very dull and boring if you were not here. But I have to be practical."

"That is an extremely boring word," he complained. "Like 'sensible', 'reasonable' and of course 'doing one's duty'."

Lucille laughed because she could not help it.

But, as they ate their delicious luncheon and drank most of the champagne, she had the distinct feeling that she was gambling with her future.

When they had finished their luncheon, Lucille threw the scraps that were left over outside so that the birds could enjoy them.

Meanwhile the Marquis tossed the bottle of champagne deep into the bushes, where it would not be found.

Then, as Lucille went back into the Folly for her jacket and hat, he followed her, saying,

"Tell me you enjoyed our picnic together."

"Enormously."

"Then we can do it again?"

The Marquis spoke eagerly and she turned her head away from him and stood at the opening in the wall.

She looked out at the sunshine before she said,

"I think it is time you returned to London."

"I have no intention of leaving you!"

She did not reply and after a moment he exclaimed,

"Oh, for God's sake, Lucille, you know I am in love with you! It's impossible for me to think of anything else and, when you are not here, you haunt me."

Very slowly she turned her face towards his.

"What – are you – saying?"

"Must I say it again?" he replied. "I love you and I want more than I have ever wanted anything in the whole of my life to kiss you."

He put out his arms towards her, but she moved away from him.

"No."

"Why not?"

"Because I have – never been kissed – and I know – instinctively that it would be – a mistake."

"A mistake for whom?" the Marquis demanded.

"For me – and, as we are – alone here – I have to look after – myself."

"How can you say such things?" the Marquis asked. "I will look after you and I promised not to hurt you. But I love you, Lucille, and I have to see you. I have to be with you."

Again he tried to put his arms around her, but Lucille turned away.

Then she picked up her jacket and hat and walked towards the door.

He did not follow her. He only stood watching her until, just as she was about to step outside, he asked,

"Where are you going?"

"Home."

"Why?"

There was a little pause and then Lucille turned back to face him.

"Because," she said slowly, "what was light-hearted and – fun is becoming – serious and that is a – mistake!"

"It is not a mistake where I am concerned," the Marquis answered, "and I know exactly what you are saying to me and what you are thinking."

She raised her eyes to his and they gazed at each other without either of them moving.

Then very quietly the Marquis said,

"This is something I have never done before, but I am asking you, Lucille, to marry me!"

*

The double doors opened and the butler announced,

"Lord Kenyon Shaw, my Lady,"

The Countess of Dulwich rose with a little cry from the chair where she had been sitting as her brother came into the room.

"Kenyon!" she exclaimed. "I heard only last night that you were back and I cannot tell you how glad I am to see you."

They moved towards each other, and Lord Kenyon kissed his sister's cheek and said with a smile,

"Your note told me that you needed me urgently. What has happened? Has my most estimable brother-in-law run away with a ballet dancer?"

"No, of course not!" the Countess exclaimed in shocked tones. "Lionel would not think of doing anything so reprehensible!"

Then she realised that her brother was teasing her and said,

"You look extremely well, Kenyon, if very thin. What have you been doing with yourself?"

"Actually it was very hot in India and I was rather busy or I would have been here sooner."

He seated himself as he spoke in a comfortable armchair.

Looking at him, the Countess thought that it would be impossible for any man to look so handsome or more attractive.

The third Marquis, their father, had had four children, two boys and two girls, all four of whom were outstandingly good-looking.

In fact the girls had been acclaimed as beauties and both had made exceptionally satisfactory marriages.

The youngest member of the family, Lord Kenyon, was thirty-three.

He had been spoilt and idolised by his sisters since the moment he was born.

This also applied, if all the reports could be believed, to a great number of other beautiful women as well.

But Lord Kenyon had had no intention once he left Eton of living the Social Life that enthralled his sisters.

He had also not emulated his elder brother, the fourth Marquis, who had been in the Diplomatic Service.

He had become a soldier and had found in India that his 'special duties', as they were called, enthralled him so completely that he seldom returned to England.

Now he was home for no apparent reason and his sister, almost as if she was prompted, asked him,

"What brought you back?"

"That is a question I cannot answer."

"Then I suppose that means you have been in danger again! Lionel told me how brilliantly you have helped the Viceroy and that you would have been awarded half-a-dozen medals if it had not all been so secret."

"Lionel should keep his mouth shut!" Lord Kenyon said sharply.

"I can assure you that Lionel is discretion itself," the Countess retorted, "and what he has said has been for my ears only."

"Whatever you may know, don't talk about it," her brother admonished her.

"I would not do anything so foolish," the Countess said. "But to be honest it has been dangerous, has it not?"

"At times very," Lord Kenyon admitted. "So for the moment I have been advised to return home and lie low and that answers your original question as to why I am here."

The Countess gave a deep sigh.

"I suppose what you have been doing is worthwhile and I only hope that the Empire is grateful. But if anything happened to you, Kenyon, I think it would break my heart."

"Well, for the moment I am safe and sound."

He spoke lightly.

He thought as he did so that in this last exploit in what the British in India called *The Great Game*, he had missed death by no more than a split second.

When he had been hurried out of India, he knew that he was a 'marked man'.

No one except for the Viceroy and the Chiefs of Staff knew how in disguise he had infiltrated into Afghanistan.

There he had discovered much of the Russians' plans to cause trouble along the North-West Frontier and that this was intended to facilitate their invasion of India itself.

His discoveries had been an undoubted triumph.

He had been congratulated behind closed doors and the Viceroy had told him,

"If justice was done, you would receive the greatest honour that the Queen Empress Victoria could bestow on you. As it is, Shaw, we can only thank you from the bottom of our hearts for saving the lives of our soldiers and perhaps India herself."

It was with those words ringing in his ears that Lord Kenyon had come home.

After all he had been through, he could not help wondering with amusement what small domestic problem had upset his sister.

She had sent him a note the moment he arrived in London.

She had said that it was of the utmost urgency that she should see him immediately.

Before he could ask any further questions, however, the door opened.

The grey-haired butler, who had been with the Countess ever since she married, brought in a silver tray with a bottle of champagne on it.

He poured out a glass for Lord Kenyon and his sister accepted only a mouthful before the servant withdrew.

Lord Kenyon raised his glass and toasted,

"To you, Charlotte, and it is good to be back."

He drank a little of the champagne.

Then he set the glass down on a small table beside him and said,

"Now, tell me what all this is about."

"It is about Marcus, which I am sure will not surprise you."

Lord Kenyon smiled.

"What has the boy been up to now? I expect he is 'sowing his wild oats' and that is something you must allow him to do."

"Wild oats!" the Countess exclaimed. "You have no idea, Kenyon, how badly he has behaved."

"Tell me about it," her brother suggested.

He settled himself more comfortably in his chair as he was thinking that his sisters always made a fuss about nothing.

It was to be expected that his nephew, who had inherited the title at the age of twenty-two, should immediately attempt to 'set the town on fire'.

When his sister-in-law, the Marchioness of Shawforde, left her husband and took her son with her, she had brought him up in Northumberland.

He had Tutors, but to the annoyance of the family he had not been allowed to go to Eton as his father and uncle had done.

Instead, he had been sent to what his mother considered a suitable school in Edinburgh and it was understood that there discipline was more severe than in any school in the South.

Lord Kenyon was a good judge of men.

His exploits would not have been so brilliant if he had not had an acute perception and he had, therefore, expected that once his nephew was twenty-one and his own Master, he would rebel.

The restrictions forced upon him ever since he had been a small boy would have been tedious for anyone.

He had not been mistaken, but Marcus had not actually been free until his father died.

Aged twenty-two he had become the fifth Marquis of Shawforde and his mother could no longer restrain him.

Lord Kenyon therefore listened good-humouredly while his sister related first the scandals that Marcus had caused in London.

There had been parties and, of course, women, ranging from the Ballet dancers of Drury Lane to the beautiful Lady Swinneton, who it appeared found him very engaging.

There was indeed very good reason for her husband to be incensed.

It was exactly what Lord Kenyon had expected would happen and then his sister said,

"Now I have even worse to tell you and I know you will be as shocked as I am!"

"Worse?" Lord Kenyon enquired.

"I have been arranging for some time," the Countess continued, "that Marcus should marry the daughter of the Duke and Duchess of Cumberland."

She paused before she explained,

"You will remember that Emily Cumberland has always been a great friend of mine and her daughter is as attractive as she was, a charming girl with delightful manners and the outstanding *debutante* of the year."

"And what had Marcus to say to this?" Lord Kenyon enquired.

"He agreed with me that it would be a good match, especially as Sarah is an excellent rider to hounds and Marcus, like all the Shawfordes, is outstanding on a horse."

"Then what has gone wrong?" Lord Kenyon asked her.

"Marcus and Sarah were to announce the engagement at a dinner party I was giving this week, but he went to the country ten days ago and has not yet returned."

The Countess saw that her brother looked puzzled and added,

"I am told on good authority that he is in the clutches of some country wench who lives near The Hall and, although I can hardly believe it, he is infatuated with her."

"A country wench?" Lord Kenyon exclaimed. "That does not sound like his taste in the female line up to date."

The Countess did not smile.

"Do be sensible, Kenyon!" she reacted sharply. "The boy is impulsive and might easily be carried away by a girl who is different from those he has met in London."

Her voice sharpened as she went on,

"If she is scheming and perhaps clever enough, she might persuade him to marry her."

"I am sure that would be a great mistake," Lord Kenyon said.

"A mistake?" his sister cried, her voice rising. "It would be a disaster! You know as well as I do that the Shaws, while they may have many faults, have never all down history soiled or defamed our lineage."

As if she thought that her brother was not impressed, she said,

"There have been a few scandals, as you well know. Your great-uncle kept an actress for many years, but he did not marry her."

Her voice was filled with pride as she continued,

"If you look at the Family Tree, you will find that the wife of every Marquis has been of the same social standing as himself."

As if she knew what her brother was thinking without his putting it into words, the Countess went on,

"Of course, I realise that Marcus's mother behaved disgracefully in leaving George as she did, but at least she was the daughter of an Earl and so exceedingly rich that I suppose we must forgive her."

"I am not disputing that Marcus is well-bred," Lord Kenyon said, "and when I last saw him I thought that he was an intelligent young man. I just cannot believe that he would be so stupid as to make a *mésalliance* with some young woman we would be ashamed of."

"That is exactly what he is doing," the Countess said, "and that is why I sent for you. There is no one else who could speak to Marcus as you could."

"Why me?" Lord Kenyon enquired.

"Oh, don't be stupid, Kenyon," his sister said. "Marcus has always admired you ever since he was a small boy."

Lord Kenyon smiled a little mockingly but did not interrupt the flow.

"I wrote to him regularly," the Countess went on, "although I was seldom able to see him when he was kept in the North all those years, but the only member of the family who ever did anything interesting was you."

Lord Kenyon frowned.

"I hope you have not been indiscreet!"

"No, no! I said only how much you were appreciated in India and, when he came to see me after arriving in London, the first person he asked about was you."

The Countess was about to say and then checked herself that Marcus had in fact asked blithely,

"What is Uncle Kenyon up to now? I have heard in the Club that he is a past Master at disguise and the Russians are after his blood!"

It was the sort of remark that the Countess knew would infuriate her brother.

She therefore merely added,

"Because he never saw his father, he looks up to you and that is why only you can talk to him."

"I must say you make me feel my age," Lord Kenyon said. "You seem to have forgotten that George was twenty years older than I am and I really don't believe that I can appear as a *Paterfamilias* to his son."

"However you appear is not important," the Countess retorted sharply. "What you have to do, Kenyon, is to go to The Hall and find out what is happening."

"It is something I have no wish to do."

The Countess ignored her brother's remark, saying,

"If that young woman really has her claws into Marcus, we will have to pay her off."

"How do you know that your theory is true?" Lord Kenyon enquired.

There was silence as the Countess was considering whether or not she should tell him the truth.

Then she said,

"As it happens, my lady's maid, who has been with me for over thirty years, is the sister of Jones, the Head Housemaid at Shaw Hall. You may remember Jones, a rather gaunt woman who disapproved of almost everything, but was excellent at her job."

"I might have guessed that what you heard was servants' gossip," Lord Kenyon said scornfully.

"Jones is hardly a servant. She is almost one of the family, having been with us for so long. She kept the house together when George was always away in some outlandish place in the East."

With a warmth in her voice she finished,

"When I stayed at the house for his funeral, I found that nothing was changed. Everything was just as it was in Mama's day and that was all due to Jones."

"And did Jones say who this woman is?"

"Yes. Her name, now let me think, her name is Winterton."

The Countess frowned before she went on,

"I seem to remember the Wintertons, but I am not certain. Anyway they are obviously not of any consequence."

She made a gesture with her hands.

"It would be a disaster, a complete and absolute disaster, for Marcus to marry some young girl who would not know how to behave as the Marchioness of Shawforde."

"I agree with you there," Lord Kenyon nodded. "And we certainly don't want a divorce in the family or another separated couple like George and his wife."

"How can you think of anything so terrible?" the Countess cried in alarm. "A divorce would be a humiliation for us all!"

"It is extremely inconvenient, just as I have arrived home," Lord Kenyon said, "but I will go down to The Hall tomorrow to see Marcus and find out what is going on."

He sighed and rose to his feet.

"I expect it will all be a 'storm in a tea cup' and Marcus's intentions, if he has any, are strictly dishonourable."

"I can only hope you are right," the Countess asserted fervently. "Thank you, dear Kenyon, I knew I could rely on you to save us."

CHAPTER THREE

After the Marquis had asked Lucille to marry him, she stared at him for a long moment.

It was as if she did not understand what he was saying.

Then, as he moved towards her, she stammered somewhat incredulously,

"D-did you – ask me to – marry you?"

He put his arms around her.

"I love you," he insisted. "I love you so much that it is quite different from anything I have ever felt before."

She gazed at him, but she did not speak.

Surprisingly gently he kissed her.

It was almost as if he was afraid to touch her lips.

Then, when he did so, a little quiver ran through Lucille.

They clung together like two children who had been frightened in the dark and suddenly felt safe again.

The Marquis kissed her until finally she turned her head, saying,

"No – please – no!"

"Why not?" he asked. "This is the most wonderful thing that has ever happened to me."

"Because – you should not – marry me."

"I have every intention of marrying you!" he said in a firm voice that he had not used before.

"B-but Delia told me that you are – engaged to somebody – else."

The Marquis's arms tightened around her.

"If I was engaged or married to fifty women, I would still want only you!"

His voice was like a trumpet call ringing out around the Folly.

Lucille thought that it was as if he had suddenly grown older and more of a man than he had been since she had known him.

Because she felt, however, that she should concentrate on what was important, she asked,

"Is it – true that – you are – engaged?"

"I am not engaged," the Marquis replied angrily. "But my aunt has been trying to push me into marriage ever since my father died."

"And you – agreed?"

"I said I would think about it," the Marquis averred, "and I promised to attend a dinner party where the girl would be present, but that is all."

Lucille moved from his arms.

Then she felt as if her legs would not carry her, so she sat down on the step where they had eaten.

The Marquis sat beside her.

He was looking at her and she thought that the expression in his eyes was very revealing.

He lifted her hand and kissed it, saying,

"I love you so overwhelmingly that nothing and nobody shall stop me from making you my wife."

"We have to – think about – it."

"Why? What is there to think about?" the Marquis asked. "I love you and I think you love me. We will be very happy."

He smiled before he added,

"I shall become such a good and compassionate landlord that you will be very proud of me!"

"I am proud of you now because you are trying," Lucille answered. "But Delia is right. Your family would – never accept – me."

To her surprise the Marquis laughed.

"They have never accepted or bothered about me until my father died."

"I heard you had lived in the North," Lucille murmured.

"I was more or less imprisoned there by my mother," the Marquis said, "and when my family thought that my father would live, as he should have done, to an old age only Aunt Charlotte bothered to keep in touch with me."

"Surely that was very unkind?" Lucille enquired.

"'Indifferent' is the right word until they thought that they might get something out of me."

"That is cynical."

"I don't feel cynical," the Marquis said. "It only amused me how they toady to me now because I am very rich, besides being the Head of the Family."

Lucille did not answer.

She turned her head away from him and after a moment he asked anxiously,

"What are you thinking?"

"I am thinking that perhaps it is right, as Delia said, for aristocrats to marry aristocrats. Although my father was very proud of his antecedents, I suppose they cannot be compared with – yours."

"I am not marrying your antecedents," the Marquis pointed out, "but *you*!"

Lucille sighed.

"I know exactly what they are – going to say."

"And what is that?"

"First, that because you are so grand you should have an arranged marriage to the Duke's daughter or whoever she is and secondly that I am too young to know my own mind."

The Marquis put his arms around her.

"You do love me, dearest Lucille?" he asked. "Promise me that you love me because I am me and not because I am a Marquis."

"I love you because you are the most attractive man I could ever imagine," Lucille replied, "but I know they will say that I have not had enough experience of men."

"Who are 'they'?"

"Well, I suppose really, since Papa and Mama are both dead, Delia, my sister. There is no one – else to look after me."

"I will look after you," the Marquis said fiercely, "and if your sister persuades you to go to London, then I may lose you."

"Perhaps that – would be a – good thing!" Lucille answered provocatively.

He put his fingers under her chin and turned her face up to his.

"Listen," he said, "from the moment we saw each other we both knew that something had happened to us and it is something that has never happened to me before."

Lucille drew in her breath as if she felt the same and he went on,

"You are mine and I will kill anyone who tries to take you from me!"

He spoke violently.

Because he was so sincere, Lucille felt her heart leap. This was what she had always wanted to find, a man who was forceful and dominating.

The Marquis was very unlike the ineffectual rather feeble youths whom Delia had asked to dinner.

She remembered when she had come home for the holidays that she had met them out hunting and at the few parties to which she had been invited.

She had always rather despised them when they looked at her with what she called 'sheep's eyes'.

She thought that on the whole they compared unfavourably with the brothers of the French girls and she had met them when she had been invited out from school by her close friends.

The Marquis was different.

It was not just that he was good-looking and had an aura about him because of his position in life.

There was, as he had said, some link between them that they both felt.

She had felt it from the very first moment when they had met on the Racecourse.

Since then it had increased and grown every moment they had been together.

"What are you thinking?" the Marquis asked again as if he felt that she was opposing him.

"I was thinking that if we – are to be – together," Lucille replied, "we will have to be very clever about it."

"Why can we not just go back and tell your sister that we are engaged?"

"Because if we do that," Lucille answered, "I am quite certain that Delia will take me away."

"Take you away!" he exclaimed.

"Because we have always been so close," Lucille explained, "I can read her thoughts and I knew the first night after we met, when she was giving me a lecture about not seeing you again, that she was thinking that if I did not agree she would take me away."

"That is something we must prevent," the Marquis declared.

"That is why we have to be – careful not to make her – suspicious."

Lucille gave a deep sigh.

"At the same time we cannot go on for ever living in a 'Fool's Paradise' and believing that no one is – aware of what we are – doing."

"What do you mean?"

"I mean that the village has eyes everywhere and, sooner or later one of the servants, if no one else, will tell Delia that we are seeing each other."

She spoke in a worried tone and the Marquis put his arms around her and drew her close to him.

"If you think anyone can take you from me, or I could lose you, you are very much mistaken!"

His lips were against the softness of her cheek as he went on,

"I agree that we have to think and be clever about everything, because the only thing that really matters is that you should marry me."

His lips found hers and there was no need for any more words.

He kissed her until they were both breathless.

Lucille felt that Krishna the God above them was playing on his pipes because they were so happy.

Only when the excitement and rapture that the Marquis had ignited in her was too overpowering to be borne did she hide her face in his neck.

She then found that his heart was beating as tumultuously as hers.

*

Lord Kenyon left London early the next morning.

He was driving a chaise that belonged to his nephew and four outstanding well-bred chestnuts.

He thought it surprising that Marcus had not taken them with him to The Hall.

Then he learned that the party who had been at The Hall two weeks ago had travelled there by train and it was actually a more complicated journey than by road.

Lord Kenyon had a good idea of the type of parties his nephew was giving.

He was, therefore, aware that the over-painted women in their feathers and silks would be more comfortable in a private coach.

It would have been attached to the train at Euston Station and food and drink could be served during the journey.

What Lord Kenyon was enjoying as he drove was the cool air on his face and the sunshine in his eyes that was never, as it was in India, overwhelming.

He was a very proficient driver and, although it was some time since he had driven a four-in-hand, he had not lost his skill.

The groom sitting beside him watched in admiration at the way he tooled his team through the traffic. He let the horses have their heads as soon as they reached the country.

It took only two hours to reach the impressive wrought iron gates that led to Shaw Hall.

As he drove up the avenue of ancient oaks, he thought it strange to be coming back.

The Hall had been his own home when he was a small boy, but otherwise he had spent very little time there.

Soon after he went to a Boarding School his father died and his elder brother George had inherited the title and estate.

He thought as he drove on what a disaster George's marriage had been.

It had also been a mistake that Marcus had been brought up in a different way from the rest of the family.

He should have gone to Eton, then to Oxford University and, more important than anything else, into a smart Regiment.

There had been Shaws who had served in the Life Guards and others in the Grenadiers and he knew that Marcus would have been welcomed into either of those Regiments.

Instead of which his mother had kept him in the North where, from all reports, he had led a very restricted life.

It was quite obvious, Lord Kenyon reflected, that once he was free he would enjoy himself.

It was bound to be considered 'outrageous' and there was no one to blame but his mother, who was now dead.

Lord Kenyon had always thought her tiresome and puritanical and that she was immensely rich would not really compensate Marcus for the years when he had no chance of making the right friends.

More importantly he had missed the discipline and comradeship he would have found in a Regiment.

'I feel sorry for the poor boy,' Lord Kenyon told himself.

Equally he was convinced that his sister was right.

An unfortunate marriage would be a disaster, not only for Marcus himself, but for the rest of the family.

Lord Kenyon was well aware what women could be like when they wished to get a man into their clutches and to marry him.

There had been a number of women in his life.

The majority of them had been charming sophisticated ladies. With them he had delightful *affaires de coeur* with no hard feelings on either side when it was over.

But there had been one or two who had been difficult. They had pursued him relentlessly and had been determined that he should marry them.

He felt a shudder go through him.

He remembered how on several occasions he had had to extract himself with the same dexterity he had shown when dealing with the Russians.

It had not been easy.

The alternative had been to have a millstone in the shape of an undesirable woman around his neck for life.

'The boy is too young and too inexperienced to know how to deal with women like that,' Lord Kenyon ruminated.

There was a squareness about his chin and a hard look in his eyes.

And he knew that he must save Marcus, however disagreeable it might be for him personally.

*

The Hall was looking, Lord Kenyon thought, more impressive than usual.

He saw that the sun was shining and glistening on the windows and appeared to welcome him with a wide golden smile.

Often in India when he was sweltering in the almost unbearable heat of the plains or crawling through rocks and gullies on a cold night on the North-West Frontier, he would have a vision of The Hall.

He would see its green lawns, its white and purple lilac in blossom, and the lake, smooth and unruffled as a mirror.

Then he would know that he must survive so that he could return to England and enjoy again the beauty of it.

He had a house of his own which he had every intention of visiting as soon as possible.

It was, however, in Somerset, and he had a great deal to do first in London. In fact his sister Charlotte had disrupted what had been a well-thought-out programme.

He was aware that he must make a call at the India Office, where he had a great deal of information that they were waiting to hear.

After which the Prime Minister, the Marquis of Salisbury, would, if he knew that he was back home, demand his presence.

There was too the uncomfortable feeling that Queen Victoria would be annoyed if he did not visit her at Windsor Castle at the first opportunity.

He could only hope, therefore, that his mission on behalf of the family would not take him long.

'I will make it quite clear to the young woman that there is no question of Marcus marrying her,' he told himself.

And a little farther down the road he added,

'If she is at all difficult then, as Charlotte suggested, a large sum of money will doubtless assuage what she will doubtless call her 'broken heart'.'

He drove his horses over the bridge that spanned the lake to the great house that was just ahead of him.

As he did so, he thought that the Marchioness of Shawforde must be someone worthy to step into his mother's place.

His mother had been loved, admired and respected by everybody.

From the Queen, who had made her one of the Ladies of the Bedchamber, down to the old pensioners living in the alms-houses built by his grandfather.

Even the children who attended the school in the village, which had also been provided by his grandfather, had adored her.

As Lord Kenyon stepped down from the chaise, two footmen had run a red carpet down the steps. Then the butler, whom he remembered, appeared at the top of them.

"Good morning, Jones," he said, holding out his hand.

"Good morning, my Lord. This is indeed a surprise," the butler replied.

"I know," Lord Kenyon admitted, "but I have just returned to England and I want to see his Lordship."

"I'm afraid, my Lord, that you'll be disappointed."

"Disappointed?" Lord Kenyon enquired.

"His Lordship's gone out for the day. He is, if I might say so, exploring the estate and he has taken with him a packed luncheon."

Lord Kenyon stood still in the hall, thinking over what the butler had just said.

Then he replied,

"In that case, as I have a call to make in the village, I will go there first and I should be glad if I could have luncheon when I return."

"Of course, my Lord, that'll be arranged and perhaps your Lordship'd fancy a glass of wine now?"

"No, thank you, Jones. I don't expect to be long."

He turned to see that his chaise was just being driven away to the stables and stopping it, he took the reins from the groom.

As he drove back down the drive, he had deliberately not said where he was going.

He was aware that with their usual curiosity, the servants would all discuss it the moment his back was turned.

Instead he drove to the drive gates, stopped and said to his groom,

"Ask the lodge keeper to come and speak to me."

"Yes, my Lord."

The man was just about to obey his order, when on an impulse Lord Kenyon remarked,

"You come from these parts, do you not?"

"I does, my Lord, but his Lordship asked me to come up to London 'cos they were short-staffed."

"Then there is no need to bother the lodge keeper," Lord Kenyon said. "You will know where the Wintertons live."

"Yes, my Lord, I does," the groom replied. "Straight up the village and the house be on the left."

Lord Kenyon asked no more questions.

He let the groom direct him until they came to some gates that he vaguely remembered. There were no lodges and the gates themselves stood open leading into a drive bordered on each side by rhododendron bushes.

It was not a long drive.

At the end of it was what Lord Kenyon appreciated as an ancient Elizabethan Manor House.

It was not very large, but in perfect preservation. The bricks had over the years mellowed to a soft pink and its diamond-paned windows made it exceedingly attractive.

Lord Kenyon drew his horses to a standstill outside what was obviously the front door.

Handing the reins to his groom, he stepped out.

Now there was no footman here to run down the red carpet.

He pulled the iron bell, but nobody came to the open door and after a moment's hesitation, he stepped into the hall.

He noticed that the panelling was of the same period as the house, as was the carved oak staircase.

The door to what he imagined would be the main room opposite him was half-open and he walked towards it.

He thought it strange that there should be no sign of any servants.

*

Delia had left the front door open when she had come in from the garden.

She had been picking flowers and was now arranging them.

The vases and bowls all had their traditional places in the drawing room since her mother had first decorated it.

"I cannot bear a room without flowers," she had said, "and I know, although he does not always say so, that they make your father happy."

Delia was to learn as she grew older that anything her mother did made her father feel happy.

For him the sunlight had gone from the house after her death

No amount of flowers or anything Delia might do could compensate him for losing the woman he loved.

Delia, however, was vividly conscious that her mother was not dead, but still with them.

Sometimes she would feel her so close that she would talk to her about her problems.

And it was something that she was doing now.

She was asking her mother's help in arranging the Flower Show in the village. It was an occasion that was very important to Little Bunbury.

It was one of the duties that Delia had undertaken after her mother had died and every year it gave her great concern.

One difficulty was to prevent the gardeners at The Hall from walking off with every prize as the other competitors not only resented it, but felt discouraged from competing.

This year she had inaugurated a large number of competitions in which the large houses in the neighbourhood could not compete. There was a special prize for the best marrow from a cottage garden.

This was because last year Mrs. Geary had been very voluble.

Her vegetable marrow had outweighed and been larger than that entered by the Head Gardener of The Hall.

The judge, however, according to her, had deliberately chosen the entry that went under the Marquis's name.

"I knows that judge," she had said bitterly. "A real snob, 'e be! Always toadyin' to them as 'as a title and it's not fair, Miss Delia, that it ain't. So you'll 'ave no vegetable marrow from me this year!"

It took all Delia's tact and charm to persuade Mrs. Geary that they could not possibly have the competition without her.

Delia had extended her idea of organising competitions exclusively for those who lived in the village cottages.

She had suggested one for arrangements of wild flowers in which the schoolchildren could compete. Another was for the prettiest collection of leaves and grasses.

This had caused a great deal of surprise, but almost everybody in the village could enter.

As usual, when she concentrated on what she was doing, Delia arranged her flowers automatically.

She was hardly seeing them, but thinking of the Flower Show and, of course, of Lucille.

Actually she was not particularly worried about her sister.

Recently she had seemed so much more content than she had been when she first came home.

She had been busy, or so she told Delia, calling on all her old friends in the locality.

Some of them lived at the other end of the County.

Because Delia was so occupied she had accepted Lucille's suggestion that she should ride off every morning.

She usually announced,

"Don't expect me back to luncheon, dearest, because they are sure to beg me to stay with them and it is quite a long ride."

'At least,' Delia thought complacently, 'she is amusing herself until she can go to London. I only wish I could spare the time to accompany her, but I must finish the Flower Show first.'

She was wondering whether everybody had the place for their stall where they had had it last year, also if there would be enough room in the marquee for another village, which had joined them.

The Flower Show had originally been for the inhabitants of Little Bunbury.

Then Great Bunbury, which was about two miles away and Water End, about the same distance in the opposite direction, joined in.

Now another village had begged permission to take part and Delia found that she could not refuse.

"We may be rather crowded," she said to the Vicar.

"I have thought of that," he replied, "but if it is a fine day, most people will be happy to be out of doors, and, of course, Miss Delia, admiring your beautiful garden."

The Flower Show always took place in the paddock at The Manor and one of the joys of the afternoon was to walk through the Rose Garden, explore the shrubberies and sit on the green lawns.

Tea was provided by willing helpers and it demanded a great deal of preparation on Delia's part.

She could always rely on a number of people to help her, but she recognised that everything had to be carefully organised or otherwise there would be chaos.

She finished the last vase of flowers with relief.

She was just thinking that she should now find out if the men had arrived with the marquee, when somebody came into the room.

She looked up and realised with surprise that it was a complete stranger.

"Please forgive me," he said when he saw her, "but I have been ringing the bell and there has been no answer, so I have walked in."

"Oh dear, I am afraid it has broken again," Delia exclaimed. "And the servants are all busy in the kitchen."

She knew that what was keeping them busy was that she had told them to sort out the cups and saucers.

These were always kept, year after year, in the cellar and, when the Flower Show came round, they had to be washed.

"Would it be possible for me to see Mr. Winterton?" Lord Kenyon asked.

"I am afraid my father is dead," Delia replied.

This was something that Lord Kenyon had not expected and he looked surprised for a moment.

"I am sorry. May I talk to you instead?"

"Yes, of course."

She was thinking as she looked at him that he was not only extremely handsome but very smartly dressed.

She was wondering who he could possibly be, when he said,

"Perhaps I should introduce myself. My name is Shaw – Lord Kenyon Shaw."

Delia drew in her breath.

Now she realised who he was and she said,

"Will you please sit down? I suppose you have only recently come back from India."

"You know that I was in India?" Lord Kenyon enquired.

"I think you were the only relative who was not present at your brother's funeral."

"It was impossible for me to get away in time," Lord Kenyon replied vaguely, "and I returned home only the day before yesterday to receive rather worrying reports about my nephew, the present Marquis, which is why I came to see your father."

Delia looked surprised and then, as Lord Kenyon seated himself in a chair by the fireplace, she sat opposite him.

It flashed through her mind that perhaps he had heard of his nephew's disgraceful parties at The Hall and he had therefore come to ask her father what was the reaction of the village to such behaviour.

There was a little pause as if Lord Kenyon were choosing his words carefully.

Then he said,

"I understand, Miss Winterton, that my nephew, despite the fact that he is engaged to be married, has become somewhat involved with you!"

Delia stared at him incredulously.

Then she realised first that he had mistaken her for Lucille and secondly what he was implying.

She had trusted Lucille completely and she thought that she had accepted her direction that she should not see the Marquis again.

Now for the first time a suspicion that she had been deceived occurred to her.

At the same time her immediate impulse was to protect Lucille.

"I don't know – what your Lordship means," she prevaricated.

"Come now, Miss Winterton," Lord Kenyon replied, "I have been told on good authority that you and my nephew have been constantly in each other's company and this, you must be aware, is extremely reprehensible when he is engaged."

"I did hear," Delia said quietly, "that the Marquis was to be betrothed and therefore I think that your Lordship must be mistaken in what you have just averred."

"I think not, Miss Winterton," Lord Kenyon said, "although, of course, if I have been misinformed, I will apologise. However, I would like your assurance or, if you prefer, your word of honour, that you and my nephew mean nothing to each other."

This, Delia thought, was something that she could give him in all sincerity.

But she was afraid for Lucille and was not quite certain what she should do.

After a few second's hesitation she said tentatively,

"I think it would be fairer, my Lord, if you told me exactly what you have heard about your nephew's intentions and what you suspect is being done about it."

"Very well, Miss Winterton, if that is what you want," Lord Kenyon replied. "The truth is that my sister has been told that you are trying to marry my nephew, which, as you must be aware, would be, from his point of view, an utter disaster."

He spoke so scathingly that Delia felt her anger rising.

He could not have been ruder, Delia thought, if Lucille came from the gutter.

She did belong to a family who had been respected for nearly as long as his own and, as far as her father was concerned, he had served his country as a soldier in the same way that Lord Kenyon had.

"I think, my Lord," she said quietly, "that you are being unnecessarily insulting. If what your sister has heard is true, it might, from the point of view of your family, be unfortunate, but it would certainly not be the disaster you have suggested."

There was a silence.

And then Lord Kenyon said,

"I assure you I did not mean to be rude, Miss Winterton. At the same time you must be aware that the Marquis of Shawforde holds an exceptional position in Society and so will his wife have, when he has one."

"That may be your opinion, my Lord," Delia replied, "and it is, of course, the conventional and traditional one. But we who live here are well aware that the late Marquis, who made the type of marriage you are advocating, was not a happy man nor was the marriage a successful one."

Delia surprised even herself by what she had said. But because Lord Kenyon had insulted Lucille, she was determined to defend her sister.

"That is true," Lord Kenyon admitted, "but you will understand that because my brother was so unfortunate, I have no wish for his son to find himself in the same position."

"I think you may find that the – present Marquis is perhaps not such an – advantageous match as his predecessors."

Lord Kenyon raised his eyebrows, but he did not speak and Delia went on,

"The Marquis has already – scandalised the people on the estate, the village and the neighbours by the – parties he has given since he inherited."

"And yet you still want to marry him?" Lord Kenyon asked.

"I have not said that I wish to marry him," Delia replied. "I am merely pointing out that the blue-blooded aristocrat you are proposing as his wife may not be as eager as you seem to think!"

"What you are saying is absolute nonsense!" Lord Kenyon retorted loftily. "The Duke and Duchess of Cumberland are delighted for their daughter, Sarah, to marry my nephew and the engagement will be announced the moment he returns to London."

He looked at Delia with what she thought was a hard expression in his eyes before he continued,

"What I am asking, Miss Winterton, is that you cease trying to persuade him to stay here in the country and instead allow him to do as his family wishes."

"And what if that is not what he wishes himself?" Delia asked.

She was arguing because she was so angry with Lord Kenyon for what he had just said.

Also because she was frantically wondering how she could extract Lucille from this unfortunate situation without her reputation being damaged.

"I am sure when I have the opportunity of speaking to my nephew," Lord Kenyon went on, "that he will do what I ask of him. After all I do not think that you can have known him for very long, Miss Winterton, and he is well aware of his duty to his family."

"That has certainly not been very noticeable since he came to The Hall," Delia said sharply, "but I am sure your Lordship will be very persuasive."

She rose to her feet as she spoke and there was nothing that Lord Kenyon could do but rise too.

"I have not come here to quarrel with you, Miss Winterton," he said in a different tone. "My intention was to appeal to your better nature."

"I think, my Lord, if you are honest, you are determined to get your own way and I can only reply that the decision, of course, rests with your nephew. I have therefore nothing further to say on the matter!"

"But you will let him go?" Lord Kenyon asked.

Delia smiled a little mockingly.

"I understand that the Marquis is twenty-three years old and has a will of his own. I would be very surprised if he proves to be a puppet for you to pull his strings and make him do exactly what you want."

"Now, listen to me, Miss Winterton – " Lord Kenyon began.

"I think, my Lord, we have nothing further to say to each other on this matter," Delia interrupted, "and, as I have a great many things to attend to, I feel that any further argument would simply be a waste of my time and yours."

Lord Kenyon was surprised to find that for the first time in his life he was at a loss for words.

He had thought when he first saw Delia that, as she seemed so young, anything he had to say to her would be easy and she would be over-awed by him.

Instead of which he realised now that in an exchange of words or rather what one might call a 'duel', she had undoubtedly come out the winner.

He had been intent on what he had to say and it was only now, as he looked at her more closely, that he realised that she was very lovely.

It was understandable that young Marcus should lose his head and perhaps his heart.

Delia stood waiting for him to leave.

He thought, as he looked at her again, that in fact she was quite unlike anybody else he had ever seen and certainly more beautiful.

She was simply dressed and yet, he thought, no Queen could have held herself more proudly.

There was something almost ethereal about her that made him think of a picture by Botticelli or music by Chopin.

Then he called himself to attention.

He remembered that this was the woman who had fastened herself onto Marcus and obviously she was determined to be the Marchioness of Shawforde.

With an effort, because he was acutely aware of how anxious Delia was for him to leave, he said,

"When I talk to my nephew, which I have been unable to do as yet, as he is not at home, may I perhaps come back to see you, Miss Winterton, and somehow arrange that you are compensated for any false hopes he has raised perhaps unwittingly?"

For a moment Delia did not understand and then her grey eyes darkened.

"I can only hope, Lord Kenyon," she said slowly, "that I never have the misfortune to meet you again!"

With that she walked away from him out of the drawing room and he was alone.

CHAPTER FOUR

Lucille came hurrying into the house from the stables and Delia was waiting for her in the drawing room.

She realised that her sister was looking very lovely. Lovelier in fact than she had seen her for a long time and she was obviously very happy.

It was something Delia thought that she ought to have noticed before.

"I am back," Lucille announced unnecessarily.

"I have been waiting to talk to you."

There was a note in Delia's voice that made Lucille feel apprehensive, but she managed to reply lightly,

"What about?"

"I trusted you." Delia answered. "It never crossed my mind that you would deceive me!"

Lucille drew in her breath.

"Oh – that –"

"Yes, that. And I am very upset."

"I was afraid you might be," Lucille replied, "but – who told you?"

"Lord Kenyon Shaw."

Lucille stared at her sister in disbelief.

"Lord Kenyon? But – how could he – I mean – where did you meet him?"

"He came here to talk to you," Delia responded, "in fact to tell you that the Marquis is engaged to be married."

"That is *not* true!" Lucille asserted. "And I cannot think how Lord Kenyon learned about us. I thought he was in India."

"He has obviously returned and he was extremely offensive."

"Offensive?" Lucille repeated in surprise.

"He insinuated that you were persuading the Marquis to stay here at The Hall rather than do his duty."

Delia spoke wearily and, as if she had to convince Lucille of the truth, she added,

"He said that marriage with you would be an utter disaster!"

To her surprise, Lucille, instead of being incensed, walked to the window.

She stood with her back to her sister and after a moment she said,

"I expect – now you will be – proved right."

"What do you mean?" Delia asked.

"Marcus has – asked me to – marry him, but – "

"Asked you to *marry* him?"

"I see no reason why you should be so surprised about it," Lucille said. "We love each other, but now that Lord Kenyon has returned things may be very different."

"Did you accept his proposal?" Delia enquired.

"I have been trying to persuade him every hour we have been together for the past week that to – marry me might be a – mistake from his point of view."

"But he loves you?"

"He says he loves me and that – nothing else matters. I thought that was true until you told me that Lord Kenyon was here."

"I do not understand," Delia said. "What has Lord Kenyon to do with it?"

"I suppose people in the country do not realise what a fantastic person he is," Lucille replied. "Marcus says that they are all talking about him in his Club."

"Why?"

"Because he has apparently carried out the most amazing exploits in India. He is part of *The Great Game* or whatever it is called. But I don't suppose you have heard of it."

"As a matter of fact Papa told me about it," Delia replied. "But are you saying that Lord Kenyon is one of the Englishmen who disguise themselves and infiltrate among the tribesmen so that we can prevent the Russians from gaining a hold on the North-West Frontier?"

"Marcus told me it was very very secret," Lucille answered, "and that we must never talk about it. To do so might harm his uncle, whom he admires more than anybody else in the whole world."

"I had no idea that Lord Kenyon was that sort of man," Delia murmured.

"Was he rude to you?" Lucille enquired.

"He was, in my opinion, very rude, not to me but to you."

She thought that Lucille did not understand and so explained,

"He came with the intention of seeing Papa. But when I told him that he was dead, he assumed that I was the Miss Winterton who was 'forcing herself' upon his nephew, very much to his detriment."

There was silence and then Lucille said,

"Well, I expect if Lord Kenyon is home – Marcus will accept whatever he advises."

"If he really loves you, whatever his relatives say would not influence him."

"He does not care about any of his relatives, none of whom paid any attention to him until he inherited the title – except for – Lord Kenyon."

There was a misery in the way Lucille spoke that touched Delia's heart.

She walked across the room to stand beside her and said as she did so,

"I am sorry, dearest, I hate you to be hurt or unhappy."

"He loves me, I know he loves me!" Lucille said. "I have only refused to come and tell you, as he wanted me to do, that we were going to be married, simply because I was thinking of him and how – disagreeable his – relatives would be – about it."

There was so much pain in her voice that Delia put her arms around her.

"I am sorry, darling, if I have made it worse," she sighed, "but I was only defending you against such cruel accusations. Lord Kenyon spoke as if we were nothing but scheming peasants!"

She thought that was a polite way of saying that what Lord Kenyon had implied was that her sister was an 'undesirable woman,' someone he thought was trying to get the Marquis into her clutches simply because of his title and riches.

She thought to say so would only make Lucille more unhappy than she was already.

She said again,

"I am sorry, darling, terribly, terribly sorry, but I was only standing up for you."

"I love Marcus," Lucille replied. "I have loved him since the first time I met him."

"You have not met many young men," Delia said gently.

"That is exactly what I thought you would say, but I think love, when it comes, is something so – overwhelming and so different from anything one has felt before – that the amount of time one has known a person means nothing."

She drew in her breath and added,

"It is as if one recognises him and has – known him before – perhaps in – another life."

Delia looked at her sister in surprise.

"Is that what you feel?"

"That is what Marcus feels. He has read a great deal about India, because he is so interested in Lord Kenyon serving there and he told me that he knew the moment he saw me that we belonged to each other and, as the Indians believe – have been together in – previous lives."

"I never thought to hear you saying anything like that," Delia observed. "I used to talk to Papa about India and I suppose I thought that you were too young to understand."

"I am old enough to be in love," Lucille sighed, "and it is very – very painful."

She gave a little cry and added,

"Oh, Delia, do you think he will go back to London and never think of me again?"

"If he does, it will mean that he is not really in love with you," Delia answered, "and it would be the best thing for you both."

"It might be the best thing for him," Lucille said in a low voice, "but – not for me. You will not believe me – but I know I shall never – love anyone else in the same way as I love Marcus."

As she spoke, she walked across the room and went into the hall without looking back.

Delia stared after her, but made no move to follow her.

She realised that Lucille wanted to be alone.

She could understand that she was suffering in a way that she had never expected anybody so young and so light-hearted to suffer.

'How could this have happened?' she asked herself. 'I suppose it is really my fault.'

On thinking back, she recognised how busy and preoccupied she had been this past week with the Flower Show.

Now that she knew that, if she had been more perceptive, she would have been aware that Lucille had been far too happy for it to be entirely natural.

'It's my fault, Mama,' she said in her heart. 'I should have looked after her better and left the Flower Show to take care of itself.'

Yet now it was too late and Lucille's heart was wounded and Delia tried to tell herself that her sister would get over it.

She had, however, the uncomfortable feeling that Lucille's feelings went deeper than she had expected them to do.

Because Delia was the elder of the two girls, after her mother's death she had taken charge of the house.

She also had to take care of her father and she had really looked upon Lucille as no more than a child.

She had, therefore, not been prepared for her to fall in love so completely with any man.

Certainly not the notorious Marquis.

'It's his fault,' she thought angrily.

Then she knew that it would be impossible to blame any man for falling in love with Lucille.

She was so unusually lovely and besides what could be more conducive to love than the fact that two young people had to meet in secret?

The whole background for love was there in the beauty of the countryside and the warm sunshine. And there was no one to interrupt them.

It was an idyll that might have come straight out of a novel.

'I should have known what was going on and stopped it,' Delia chided herself.

She had the feeling that it would have been impossible, once Lucille had met the Marquis, for her not to want to see him again.

Delia had seen him from a distance at his father's funeral and she had thought then how amazingly good-looking he was.

It had been only a fleeting glance amid the large number of mourners who had filled the small Church.

After that nobody had seen the Marquis again until stories had been reported about his outrageous behaviour in London.

These culminated in the parties that he had brought to The Hall that had scandalised the village.

'I suppose,' she thought bitterly, 'the fact that he is so raffish made him seem more attractive than he would have been otherwise.'

This was not quite true.

Having seen Lord Kenyon, she knew that the Shaws were an unusually handsome family and they certainly had no rivals locally.

Now she was frightened for Lucille, frightened that, as she said, she would never love anybody else in the same way.

While she wanted her to be happy, she felt that would be impossible with the Marquis, even if, despite his uncle's condemnation, he persisted in wanting to marry her.

It was true that Delia had not expected for a moment that the Marquis would propose marriage.

Because Lord Kenyon had been so rude and so scathing, she had felt obliged to stand up to him.

But she had thought that, if Lucille was seeing the Marquis, she would doubtless be shocked by his behaviour.

She had been wrong, completely wrong, as she had from the very beginning.

Lucille was in love and if the Marquis broke her heart, there was nothing either of them could do about it.

'I must take her away,' Delia thought frantically.

Then she remembered that if Lord Kenyon had his way, the Marquis would be taken to London.

He would then become engaged to another girl.

It was the sort of situation that Delia had never imagined would confront her and she felt frightened and unsure of herself.

Then she realised that it was time to change for dinner.

She went up the stairs slowly with a heavy heart and wondering how she could comfort Lucille.

At the same time she had to be careful not to raise any false hopes in her that the Marquis loved her enough to defy his uncle.

As she undressed, she was thinking about Lord Kenyon and it seemed strange that she had never heard before, as Lucille clearly had, that he was such a hero.

Living, so to speak, next door, she had grown up knowing all about the family. It would have been impossible not to, as the village talked of nothing else.

She was made aware of everything that happened to them from the advent of a new baby to the death of a distant relative.

She had often thought it was very unfortunate that her father had quarrelled with the last Marquis.

It was not surprising as the fourth Marquis had, after a varied career in the Diplomatic Service, come home to die although he was still only in middle-age.

He had contracted a hitherto unknown and incurable type of fever in the East, which affected his liver and it caused him bouts of pain and he was at such times confined to his bed.

He consequently became extremely disagreeable and found fault with everything and everybody and inevitably he quarrelled with his neighbours, one after the other.

Colonel Winterton was a charming man and, as a rule, easy to get along with, but he had his pride.

He was not prepared after long years of service to his country to be spoken to as if he was a raw recruit. ,

He told the Marquis what he thought of his behaviour and that ended any communication between The Hall and The Manor.

"He is a sick man, darling," Mrs. Winterton had expostulated when her husband told her what had happened.

"Sick or not the way he behaves is intolerable!" Colonel Winterton had replied. "The doctor and the Vicar have both told me that they avoid whenever possible going to The Hall because he is so exceedingly unpleasant."

"Yes, I know. Everybody in the village says the same thing," Mrs. Winterton sighed, "and it is a great pity. But I cannot imagine how he could get any better."

The Marquis actually grew worse and, when he finally died, it would have been untrue to say that anyone genuinely mourned him.

Even though they had seen very little of them during the Marquis's illness, the family was still very important to the villagers.

Delia thought it strange that no one had ever suggested that Lord Kenyon was involved in anything other than his ordinary Regimental duties.

Her father had told her about *The Great Game*, the British name for the amazing organisation of espionage that extended all over India.

Its main function was to prevent the Russians from sowing the seeds of discord among the different castes and he had told Delia, because she was so interested, how the members of *The Great Game* were known only by numbers.

It was, in fact, so secret that only the Viceroy and the Commander-in-Chief knew the identity of the men who risked their lives to preserve the British Empire.

"They must be very brave, Papa," Delia had commented.

"Very brave indeed," her father had agreed, "but it is something you must not talk about because a careless word or a whisper could cause a man's death as effectively as a bullet."

"Did you ever take part in *The Great Game*, Papa?"

There was a short pause before her father had replied to her question,

"Just once and I don't mind telling you it was one of the most frightening experiences of my life!"

"Tell me about it – please tell me," Delia had urged him.

But he had shaken his head.

"That is something I may not do. All I can tell you is that any man who takes part in *The Great Game* deserves the Victoria Cross for gallantry as no man can do more than risk his life for his country."

After what her father had said, Delia now understood.

If it was true that Lord Kenyon had been deeply involved with fighting off the Russians in the East, then it was not surprising that his nephew should hero worship him.

She put on one of her pretty evening gowns with just a slight bustle in the shape of a large satin bow at the back.

As she did so, she thought it was a pity that she could not have met Lord Kenyon in different circumstances as she would like to have talked to him about India.

It was a country that had always fascinated her from what her father had told her and in the books she had read.

She had hoped that one day perhaps she would be able to visit the country that was known as the 'Jewel in the Crown'.

'That is something that will never happen,' she thought with a little tinge of sadness.

She went downstairs pondering as to what she could say to Lucille.

It was obvious that her sister had been crying, but Delia thought it wisest not to say anything.

Soon after dinner Lucille said that she thought she would go to bed.

"I shall be glad to go to bed early too," Delia replied conversationally. "There is so much more still to arrange for the Flower Show and tomorrow the men will be erecting the marquee."

She realised that Lucille was not listening to her.

As her sister went up the stairs slowly, her head was bowed and she was walking very differently from her usual buoyant eagerness.

Delia made certain that the windows were all closed and the front door locked as old Hanson was becoming very forgetful.

She then went up the stairs to her own room.

She felt almost as depressed as Lucille and the future seemed dark and bleak.

'I *hate* Lord Kenyon!' she told herself angrily.

Equally she now understood that he was a national hero.

*

The dinner at The Hall had been excellent and was accompanied by some superb wine.

Only after they had finished did Lord Kenyon say to the Marquis,

"I want to talk to you."

Lord Kenyon had had plenty of time during the afternoon to explore the house and he found with satisfaction that everything was in perfect order.

This, of course, was due, as his sister had told him, to Jones, the butler who had been with the family almost as long as she had.

He had been aware that Jones was trying to speak to him confidentially and it was something he had no intention of doing until after he had seen Marcus.

He wanted to discover first what his feelings were towards Miss Winterton and, when he thought about her, he realised that she unexpectedly lovely.

In fact, if he had not been so angry, he would, he thought, have been astounded to find anyone so beautiful in Little Bunbury.

He could not help feeling rather uncomfortably that he had handled the whole situation badly and he should perhaps have approached her in a different way.

But his sister Charlotte had implanted so firmly in his mind that the woman who Marcus was entangled with was merely a designing minx.

So he had acted, he realised now, far too quickly and without due thought and care.

The Manor itself should have warned him that its occupant was not just some ordinary country woman seeking a rich and titled husband.

As the afternoon wore on, he walked in the garden, but he was not seeing the beauty of it, but was thinking of the anger in two large grey eyes and the graceful dignity that their owner had left the room with.

'Let's hope,' he told himself, 'that Marcus will see sense and come back with me to London.'

It was getting on for dinnertime when the Marquis finally appeared.

Lord Kenyon was in the library and his nephew, who had obviously been told of his arrival, came bounding into the room exclaiming with delight,

"Uncle Kenyon! I had no idea you were back from India."

"I arrived two days ago."

"And you have come here to see me? How splendid. I had begun to think, as I had not seen you for so long, that you were just a legend!"

"I am here and I am alive," Lord Kenyon replied with a smile. "And I am delighted to see what good shape the house is in."

There was no chance of saying anything before dinner and, after a glass of champagne, they both went up to dress.

The Marquis asked eager questions about India, which Lord Kenyon answered good-humouredly.

Now they each had a glass of brandy in front of them and Lord Kenyon thought that this was now the right moment for him to explain his real reason for coming to The Hall.

Tentatively he began,

"I hear, Marcus, that you are in some sort of trouble."

He was at once aware that the young man stiffened and there was a wary look in his eyes before he asked,

"What do you mean trouble?"

"Your Aunt Charlotte is very worried about you."

"I cannot think why."

"She had been hoping," Lord Kenyon said slowly, "that she could announce your engagement to Lady Sarah, but you have not returned to London."

"I have a good reason for remaining here," the Marquis responded quickly. "I have been getting to know the farmers and the other people on the estate."

"Is that the only reason?"

"What else did Aunt Charlotte tell you?"

"To be frank she told me that you had become involved with a young lady called Winterton and, having seen her, I can understand your interest."

"Having seen her?" the Marquis queried. "What do you mean?"

"Because when I arrived here you were out," Lord Kenyon explained, "I went to call on Miss Winterton."

"That is impossible!"

"What do you mean – impossible?"

"Because –" the Marquis began and then stopped.

He looked at his uncle for a long moment before he quizzed him,

"What exactly did you say to Miss Winterton?"

"I told her that you were engaged to be married," Lord Kenyon replied.

"That is not true!"

"Now, really, Marcus," Lord Kenyon admonished. "From what your aunt tells me, the Duke and Duchess have accepted you as a prospective son-in-law and the girl herself is, of course, agreeable."

"I have not proposed marriage to Lady Sarah and I do *not* intend to do so," the Marquis snapped. "When you meet Lucille Winterton, whom I *do* intend to marry, I hope you will understand that there is no question of there being anybody else in my life."

"I have just told you, I have met her!" Lord Kenyon reiterated.

"That is impossible since Lucille was with me the whole afternoon!" the Marquis replied.

Lord Kenyon stared at him.

"But I went to The Manor House and talked to Miss Winterton!"

"You talked to Miss Delia Winterton, who is Lucille's elder sister, and who, I may say, is entirely convinced that because of my reputation, I am not the right person for her sister to marry. In fact she has forbidden Lucille to see me."

Lord Kenyon put the glass of brandy that he had been holding in his hand down on a side table.

"I must be very obtuse," he said, "for I am finding all this very hard to understand."

"It's not difficult," the Marquis said. "Delia Winterton is exceedingly shocked by the reports of my behaviour in London and the parties I brought to The Hall, which would undoubtedly shock you too."

"I can imagine what they were like," Lord Kenyon murmured.

"But when I met Lucille," the Marquis went on, "I fell in love and I realised that she was the girl I have been looking for and whom I sincerely wish to marry."

"And she has accepted you?" Lord Kenyon asked with just a slight twist to his lips.

"On the contrary," the Marquis replied, "she is prevaricating simply because she knows that my family, who have taken no interest in me until now, would disapprove of such a marriage. And her sister, who I suppose is her Guardian, considers me beneath contempt!"

Because it was something that Lord Kenyon had not expected to hear, he could not help giving a short laugh.

"That most certainly I did not expect," he said, "and you have perturbed me by telling me that I was talking to the wrong sister!"

"I suppose you were rude to her," the Marquis remarked, "which does not help matters at all."

"Now, listen, Marcus," Lord Kenyon asserted. "It is very important not only for your own sake but also the family's that you should marry the right person – "

"That is exactly what I intend to do," the Marquis interrupted, "and, whatever you may say or think, I am absolutely convinced that it is not for you, or indeed anybody else, to choose my wife for me."

"I understood that you had met Lady Sarah," Lord Kenyon said, "and found her agreeable."

"She seemed quite a pleasant girl," the Marquis replied, "but I am not in love with her. However, I am in love with and determined to marry Lucille and nobody is going to stop me!"

He spoke in such a firm manner that his uncle looked at him in surprise.

For the first time, he realised that he was not speaking to an unfledged boy but to a man who knew his own mind.

He therefore considered it politic to play for time and in a conciliatory voice he said,

"If that is how you feel, Marcus, then it is obviously something that I must respect and I can only, of course, apologise to Miss Delia Winterton for mistaking her for her sister. I hope that you will introduce me to the right Miss Winterton tomorrow."

"That may not be so easy," the Marquis suggested.

"Why not?"

"Because, for one thing, Delia Winterton has no idea that I have been seeing her sister. So, if you told her, she now knows that she has been deceived and that is going to make things very difficult."

"I am sorry if it does," Lord Kenyon murmured.

"How could I have guessed that you would go blundering in when I have been trying to persuade Lucille to allow me to get to know her sister and hoping to improve my image in her eyes?"

"I can only apologise all round," Lord Kenyon said, "and perhaps it would be a good idea for you to come back to London and talk it over with your aunt."

"I can see exactly what you are trying to do," the Marquis exclaimed, "and that is to inveigle me away from Lucille. In the time-honoured phrase, you think we will forget each other."

He rose from the table as he continued,

"My answer is an unqualified 'no!' I am not going to leave Lucille to be snapped up by some other man and I am going to marry her just as soon as she will accept me."

As he finished speaking, the Marquis walked out of the dining room leaving his uncle staring after him in astonishment.

Outside the room the Marquis hurried down the corridor and on reaching the hall he climbed the stairs towards his own bedroom.

The Marquis's suite had traditionally been at the end of the corridor on the first floor. There were only three State bedrooms near it and the rest were in the West wing.

He thought that his uncle would probably be sleeping next to him in what was known as 'The Prince of Wales's Room,' where the later King George IV had slept on his visit to The Hall at the end of the last century.

He went quickly into his bedroom and, ringing for his valet, started to change his clothes.

He knew that somehow he had to speak to Lucille and he realised that it was not going to be easy.

He was sure that she would be upset that her sister should have learnt from Lord Kenyon that they had been deceiving her.

This was the moment when he should support her.

'I love her!' he told himself fiercely as he pulled on his riding boots. 'Nobody, not even Uncle Kenyon, is going to prevent me from marrying her.'

He had no wish to see his uncle again until he had talked to Lucille.

As soon as he was dressed, he hurried down a secondary staircase, which brought him to a door that was nearest to the stables.

They were situated on the West side of the house and they had been renovated and extended at the same time as The Hall itself.

It was easy for him to find the groom who was on night duty and he asked for the stallion he usually rode to be saddled as quickly as possible.

Then he set off across the Park.

He was aware as he did so that the remnants of the sun were crimson behind the oak trees and the first evening star was twinkling faintly in the sable of the night.

He reckoned that there would be a full moon tonight.

He wondered if he could persuade Lucille to slip away from The Manor and ride with him either into the woods or to one of the many secret places that they had found in the past week for their meetings.

'I have to talk to her,' he told himself. 'I have to persuade her that nothing matters except our love for each other.'

At the same time he was feeling very apprehensive.

He was well aware by this time of how much his parties had scandalised the village and, of course, Delia Winterton.

"I suppose," he had said to Lucille, "that your sister knows about the parties I have held here at The Hall and the way everybody behaved?"

Lucille had laughed.

"The whole village has talked about nothing else since they happened."

She looked at him from under her eyelashes and then asked,

"Did your lady guests really dance on the roof wearing nothing but their nightgowns?"

"They danced on the roof," the Marquis admitted, "but some of them were more decently covered."

Lucille laughed again.

"By the time the villagers have finished relating the tale, they will be wearing nothing!"

"I cannot think now why I was such a fool as to bring them here," the Marquis said ruefully. "If I wanted that sort of party, I could have gone to one of the hotels that cater for that sort of thing."

"Do they really?" Lucille asked in an interested tone. "Then what happens if there are two parties that are outrageous taking place at the same time?"

"That is something you should not know about," the Marquis replied, "so I am not going to talk about it."

Lucille laughed at him and teased him.

But he cursed himself for having gained a disreputable reputation, not only in London, but also in Little Bunbury.

He remembered somewhat belatedly that there was an old adage that said, *no bird should foul its own nest.*

That was what he had done.

Because Lucille was so beautiful, he wanted to keep her unspoilt and unsoiled.

He wanted to keep her in ignorance of the seamy side of life that he had once found enjoyable.

Looking back on it now, he realised it had just been an inevitable rebellion. The years of being prevented by his mother from doing anything he wanted to do had seemed endless.

He could remember that during his boyhood there had been a thousand taboos and lists of things that he might not do.

In fact there were very few things that he could do.

To be his own Master, to be very rich and to know that 'the gay life of London' was his for the taking had, of course, proved irresistible.

There were women who had fallen into his arms as soon as he looked at them, women who flattered him and made him laugh and women who taught him a thousand things he had never dreamt of before.

There had been men who wanted to drink and gamble with him, men who took him racing and introduced him to a dozen new sports he had never been allowed to attend in the North.

It was all fascinating. Yet rather, he thought now, like eating a surfeit of *pâté de foie gras* or drinking too much champagne.

Inevitably there was a headache or a hangover the next day and the feeling of regret that he had not been more abstemious.

But Lucille had understood and that was what he found so adorable about her.

She was not only young, beautiful, inexperienced and innocent, but at the same time she understood.

Perhaps because she had been educated in France, she knew that men were different from women.

A man might sow his wild oats until he loved one woman so completely that no other women existed for him.

'That is how I love Lucille,' he thought.

He now rode out of the gate at the end of the Park, which was the nearest way to The Manor.

On arrival he rode a little way up the drive and then dismounted. He tied his horsed bridle to a wooden railing and went ahead on foot.

He knew where Lucille's bedroom was and he was aware that while hers looked out on the front of the house, Delia's room overlooked the garden at the back.

She had told him so much about herself and the way they lived.

The Marquis knew that the servants would by now be comfortably asleep at the far end of The Manor. So there was no one to hear him or see him as he walked over the lawn.

He reached the gravel drive and walked until he was under Lucille's bedroom window.

He could see that a diamond-paned window was open and there was a light behind the curtains.

He whistled and, when there was no response, he whistled again.

Then the curtain was drawn back and Lucille looked out.

By now darkness had come, the stars were trembling in the sky and the moon was rising slowly above the trees.

But even if it had been pitch dark, Lucille felt that she would have known who was whistling to her.

She leaned out of the window as far as she could.

"I must see you," the Marquis said in a low voice.

Lucille nodded and pointed with her finger below her to the right where he saw that there was a door.

He waved to show that he understood and moved towards it.

Lucille went back into the room.

She had undressed and was wearing her nightgown and quickly she put over it a pretty dressing gown of blue satin that was a little paler than the colour of her eyes. It was trimmed with lace and had a number of pearl buttons that fastened it all down the front.

It was, in fact, a very demure dressing gown.

But she hesitated a moment, wondering if it would be more correct for her to dress.

Then she thought that it would be a mistake to keep the Marquis waiting.

Somebody might be aware that he was there or Delia might become suspicious and come to her room.

She had heard her sister go to bed about an hour ago and thought it unlikely and yet she did not want to take any chances.

She blew out the candles that lit her room.

She opened the door and very quietly tiptoed in her bare feet along the corridor, carrying her bedroom slippers in one hand.

She went down the stairs guided only by a faint light. It came from the ancient windows, with their heraldic shields in stained glass, which were on either side of the door.

She knew it would be wrong to open the front door. Instead, she moved in the direction that she had pointed to the Marquis.

There was a small garden door, which was easy to open and made no sound.

He was standing just outside.

Almost before she could pull the door open, he had come in and swept her into his arms.

Then he was kissing her passionately, fiercely and demandingly.

As her whole being leapt towards him, she knew that her tears had been unnecessary and so had her fear that he would no longer want her.

"I love you! *I love you!*" she wanted to shout out, but there was no need for words.

His lips told her how much he wanted her and that their love was stronger than anything else.

Only when Lucille felt that he carried her up into the sky and they were neither of them on earth did the Marquis raise his head.

"I have to talk to you, my darling," he whispered.

She closed the garden door and, taking him by the hand, she led him along a darkened corridor to a room at the end of it.

It was an attractive garden room facing South, where her mother had usually written her letters.

It was filled with the small treasures that her family had given her or which she had collected whenever she was away with her husband.

As Lucille lit the candles on the mantelpiece, the Marquis saw hanging above it a portrait of her father in uniform.

There was a fragrance of flowers and pot-pourri that Delia had made in the winter.

The candlelight illuminated the gold of Lucille's hair and the blue of her eyes as she stood looking at the Marquis.

He could only put out his arms and pull her towards him.

She was everything he wanted, and which he swore in his heart he would never lose.

"I love you and I could not go to bed without telling you so," he said in a voice that was slightly unsteady.

"I thought perhaps your – uncle would persuade you to go back to – London and – forget me," Lucille said in a very small voice.

"That is what I knew you would be thinking," the Marquis replied, "and I told him the truth."

"W-what is – that?"

"That I love you and we are going to be married!"

"Oh, Marcus – do you – mean it?"

He did not answer the question.

He merely held Lucille so tightly that it was impossible for her to breathe.

Then he was kissing her fiercely and possessively as if he would never let her go.

CHAPTER FIVE

Delia awoke from a half-sleep.

She had been dreaming that she was making out the prize tickets for the Flower Show and it was what she had been doing for most of the day.

When she was finally awake, she remembered with relief that she had finished and the Flower Show was over.

It was then she began to think once again of her conversation with Lord Kenyon.

She recognised the fact that they had fought fiercely with each other and she could feel the antagonism vibrating between them.

She felt now, however, that it was rather sad that she would never have the chance of talking to Lord Kenyon.

She would have so liked him to tell her about India that had always had an irresistible fascination for her.

Her father had told her of the years he had served in the Bengal Lancers before he married her mother and returned to England.

He had soldiered in his own country until his father died and then he thought it sensible to retire to their country home at Little Bunbury.

But he had never forgotten the beauty of India.

It had been a joy for him to serve in such a famous Regiment, noted for its horsemanship and once he had taken part in *The Great Game*.

It had seemed to Delia, when he described it, as more thrilling than anything she could read about in a book.

She had also talked to her father about the religions of India and she had found him extremely knowledgeable on the Vedas and the ancient Sanskrit writings, which totally intrigued her.

'Lord Kenyon could have told me more about all those things,' she thought with a sigh.

Instead they were at war with each other.

She forced herself to think again of the Flower Show and, as she did so, suddenly a conversation that she had hardly listened to at the time came back into her mind.

She had been working in her father's study, where she made all the arrangements for the Flower Show and she was neatly inscribing the classes in her flowing handwriting on top of the cards.

She had already written, "*1st, 2nd, 3rd, 4th,*" when Flo came into room.

Delia had looked up impatiently as Flo began,

"I'll not be disturbin' you, Miss Delia, but this be me day for doin' the brass and I likes to do it regular."

"That is all right, Flo," Delia replied, thinking that it would be a mistake to upset her.

At the same time she was hoping that Flo would work in silence as she knew only too well how garrulous she could be.

Her hope was not realised.

Flo started immediately as she picked up the brass poker,

"What do you think, miss? There's some strangers in the village and ever so strange they be!"

Delia did not reply, but that did not disconcert Flo, who continued in full flow,

"I goes into Mrs. Geary's and there they was, askin' questions about The Hall, a bit cheeky, I calls it."

She gave the poker a final polish and then atacked the tongs.

"They says as they were writin' a book about Ancestral 'omes of England, but if you asked me, I thinks they was just a couple of 'nosey parkers'!"

Delia had still not spoken and Flo continued,

"Wantin' to know everythin' about The Hall they did, 'ow many servants there was, what the State Rooms were like and even enquirin' about the bedrooms and who's sleepin' in 'em."

Flo's hand had made the brass tongs shine like a mirror before she put them down.

"That Mrs. Geary were only too 'appy to tell 'em anythin' they wants to know," she said, picking up the shovel.

"After they'd left I says to 'er, 'what do you want to go tellin' them strangers so much for?'

"'They be writin' a book',' Mrs. Geary says.

"No one can know that for sure,' I answers. "They might be burglars for all you knows'!"

"'Mrs. Geary laughs, but I says to 'er, I don't trust them foreigners and that's a fact'!"

Flo snorted and went on,

"If you'd seen 'em, Miss Delia, you'd 'ave said the same, wouldn't you now?"

She obviously was expecting a reply and then Delia asked her vaguely,

"How did you know they were foreigners?"

"No mistake about that!" Flo replied. "Black hair, black eyes, and a swarthy skin. They 'as high cheekbones and, if you asks me, they come from some Eastern country we've never 'eard of."

With that, carrying her housemaid's box containing her cleaning materials for the brass, Flo had gone from the room and with a sigh of relief Delia had once again concentrated on the Flower Show arrangements.

It was only now that Flo's story had come back into her mind.

It struck her it was indeed extremely unusual for foreigners to be in Little Bunbury and suddenly Flo's description of them made her think that they might be Russians.

It was then with a little cry that she sat up in bed.

Of course they were Russians!

They were pursuing Lord Kenyon and that was why they were interested in the bedrooms at The Hall!

Delia jumped out of bed.

Lighting a candle, she started to put on her riding skirt and the white blouse that was hanging beside it in the wardrobe.

They might laugh at her when she arrived at The Hall.

But she would warn the footman whom she knew would be on night duty that Lord Kenyon's life was in danger.

It was something that she just had to do, although she told herself that it was none of her business.

But if he was found dead in the morning, it would weigh on her conscience for the rest of her life.

Her father had made it quite clear that the men who took part in *The Great Game* gambled with death and a great number of them had died.

"That is why it has to be so secretive," he explained, "and you must never relate to anybody, my darling, what I have told you, because the Russians have long ears."

"I promise," Delia murmured as he went on,

"Once they are aware of a man's identity, he sooner or later has an unfortunate accident or simply disappears."

"It sounds terrifying, Papa."

"Yes, in a way it is. At the same time it is exhilarating to know that one is pitting one's wits against an implacable enemy who is doing his best to destroy the peace and harmony of India."

"But you might have been killed, Papa," Delia objected.

Her father had smiled.

"I would not have minded dying," he replied, "but I would very much have disliked being tortured."

"Do you mean they – torture the men they – capture?"

"Usually to try to find out more about his associates," her father answered. "That is why every man in *The Great*

Game is known by a number and has no idea of the identity of the man he is communicating with."

Because Delia had been intrigued by the whole story, she had often thought over what her father had told her.

Now she was quite sure that the two men who had been making searching enquiries of Mrs. Geary were in fact Russians.

It was obvious that they were determined to find Lord Kenyon and they would perhaps torture and then kill him.

She pulled on her riding boots and then without putting on her jacket or hat she ran down the stairs.

She reached the hall, where the only light came from the moon shining through the uncurtained windows.

She was just about to go to the front door when she suddenly noticed a light under the door of her mother's room.

Instinctively she walked towards it and opened the door.

Seated on the sofa were Lucille and the Marquis.

He had his arm around her and her head was resting against his shoulder.

For a second all three stiffened into immobility until Delia said insistently,

"Lord Kenyon's life is in danger! There are two Russians at The Hall who I think intend to kill him."

The Marquis stared at her.

Then, as he started to rise to his feet, Delia added,

"Go and saddle a horse for me! Lucille will show you the way, while I fetch my father's pistols."

She heard Lucille say something, but she did not wait to hear what it was.

She ran across the hall.

On the other side of the front door was the gun room where there was a glass-fronted cabinet and it was here that her father's sporting guns and rifles were kept along with their ammunition.

She knew that in a drawer underneath it there were three pistols, one of which he had used as an Officer. There were also two others, which were more up to date.

He had taught Delia and Lucille to shoot from the time they were quite small.

"All women should know how to defend themselves," he had said when her mother had expostulated that it was unnecessary for the girls.

Mrs. Winterton smiled.

"We are in England now, darling, not the Far East, where, I admit, it was indeed necessary."

"I taught *you* to shoot," Colonel Winterton replied, "and I think it is an accomplishment that our daughters should have too. One never knows when such skill might be necessary."

Mrs. Winterton laughed.

Her husband put up a target at the end of the lawn and then she could not resist showing off to her daughters how proficient she was.

"A bull's eye every time!" her husband commented with satisfaction.

She replied,

"I had a very good instructor."

Colonel Winterton had certainly been a good teacher where his daughters were concerned.

Both Delia and Lucille could shoot accurately and to incite them their father showed them how he could hit the right number on a playing card.

Both Delia and Lucille were determined to do the same and it was a trick that Lucille had boasted about when she was at her school in France.

One of her French friends had disbelieved her until she was invited to her Château and *she* showed off her skill with a duelling pistol to the admiration of her friend's brothers.

Delia found the pistols, as she had expected.

She took the larger one for the Marquis and a smaller one for herself.

She knew that Lucille would insist upon going with them and so she brought a third pistol for her sister.

Carrying the pistols and a supply of bullets, she went back into the hall.

As she did so, she saw through the open door the Marquis leading her horse round from the stables. And behind him came Lucille riding her favourite bay.

Delia was becoming afraid that they might be too late and that Lord Kenyon would already be dead.

She therefore did not notice that her sister was wearing only her dressing gown.

She ran towards the Marquis and handed him the pistol and bullets.

He put them into the pocket of his riding coat.

"How do you know about the Russians?" he asked, speaking for the first time.

"I will tell you about it later," Delia answered quickly. "I have only just realised what was happening."

As the Marquis spoke, he had lifted her into the saddle.

She picked up the reins and handed him the third pistol, saying,

"Give this one to Lucille."

He did as she told him and then ran ahead to where Delia saw that he had tethered his horse to a fence.

She began riding down the drive with the others following her.

On reaching the road she turned left and a few minutes later they entered the Park by the gate that the Marquis had used.

Then Delia started to ride as quickly as she dared over the rough ground.

She was thinking that if the Russians had already killed Lord Kenyon, they might meet them as they came away from the house.

She was very intent on what she was doing and she was so convinced that Lord Kenyon was in danger it had not surprised her that the Marquis had accepted her story and he had not for a moment questioned the truth of it.

They were just approaching the last of the trees before they reached the drive, when the Marquis brought his horse level with hers.

She realised a second later that he had seen a travelling carriage ahead of them.

It was coming from The Hall and just then it was crossing the bridge over the lake.

It was still some distance away.

Delia instinctively drew in her horse on the grass verge and the Marquis did the same.

"We must stop them," she whispered.

"Of course," he replied. "It's unlikely that there would be other people calling on me at this hour of the night."

"The Russians were making enquiries in the village as to where Lord Kenyon was likely to be sleeping."

She saw the Marquis's lips tighten, but he did not say anything.

His eyes were on the carriage.

It was drawn by two horses and was now approaching them.

It was then he moved into the centre of the drive and Delia followed.

A second later Lucille drew her horse up on the other side.

They stood waiting.

The moon, now high in the sky, revealed clearly that the carriage coming towards them had two men driving it.

They drove right up to them, but the riders waited, not moving.

The men were forced to draw their horses to a standstill.

One of the men said in a voice that was obviously not English,

"We want pass! We in hurry."

"I am the Marquis of Shawforde," the Marquis replied firmly, "and, as you are on my property, I wish to know who you are and where you are going."

"Get out of the way or you be sorry!" the man sitting beside the driver snarled.

As he spoke, he put his hand inside his coat.

Without waiting Delia shot him in the arm.

He gave a shriek of pain.

Before the other man could draw the gun he obviously carried from an inside pocket, Lucille shot him in the shoulder.

The Marquis had not drawn his own pistol.

Now, riding to the side of the carriage, he dismounted and opened the door.

Lying on the back seat, gagged and bound, was Lord Kenyon.

The Marquis realised that Delia had ridden her horse towards him and she was bending forward to look inside the carriage.

"Stop those men from moving," he called out sharply.

He knelt at his uncle's side and pulled off the gag.

In the moonlight he could see that Lord Kenyon's eyes were closed.

He felt his heart, afraid that he was dead.

He could, however, feel that his heart was beating and his skin was warm.

The Marquis then climbed into the carriage and he saw that Delia was holding his horse by the bridle.

The two men in the driving seat were moaning and writhing in pain.

Lucille was facing them, her pistol in her hand.

The Marquis pulled the nearest man down from the carriage and flung him roughly onto the grass verge.

He then went round to the other side and did the same to his accomplice.

When he came back to pick up the reins, Delia said in a low voice,

"I think it might be dangerous to take Lord Kenyon back to The Hall in case there are other Russians who know where he is."

The Marquis, who was just climbing onto the driving seat, stopped.

Looking at her he asked,

"What do you suggest?"

"That we take him to The Manor," Delia replied. "And I think too that it would be a mistake for the wounded men to be found here on your property."

"You are right," the Marquis agreed.

He did not, however, get onto the driving seat as Delia expected.

He walked towards Lucille, looked up at her and said,

"Your sister thinks that we should not let these devils know where my uncle will be until he recovers consciousness."

"He is – alive?" Lucille asked.

"Yes, thank God!" the Marquis replied. "I am now going to disarm these two and what I want you to do, my darling, is to stay here and stop them from leaving here until I can return. If they give you any trouble, shoot them in the leg."

"I will do that," Lucille replied, "but – please don't be – long."

"I will be as quick as is humanly possible," the Marquis answered.

They smiled at each other.

It was impossible for Delia, watching, not to realise how their faces in the moonlight expressed their love.

The Marquis had not touched Lucille, but it was almost as though he held her in his arms. Then, having taken the men's pistols, he jumped onto the driving seat of the carriage.

Delia followed, leading his horse by the bridle.

He drove back the way they had come, but slowly and carefully.

They drew up outside The Manor and Delia tethered their two horses to the wooden railings.

Then she ran to the carriage, where the Marquis was already trying to lift Lord Kenyon off the back seat.

She helped him and together they carried him into the hall.

"We can put him on the sofa," Delia said, "but later we must get him upstairs."

"Of course," the Marquis agreed.

With some difficulty, because he was a heavy man, they carried Lord Kenyon into the sitting room.

They laid him down on the sofa.

"I shall have to come back with you," Delia said, "but he will be safe here."

"Thanks to you," the Marquis said quietly.

He removed the rope that tied his uncle's legs.

Delia had, however, not waited to hear what he had to say, she hurried into the hall, where from an oak chest she drew two travelling rugs.

She brought them back into the sitting room.

As Lord Kenyon was wearing only his nightshirt, she was sure that he would be cold.

She covered him with the rugs before she followed the Marquis, who had gone to fetch their horses from where she had tethered them.

Just before she closed the sitting room door she looked back.

Lord Kenyon was covered by the rugs and had his head on a satin pillow.

He looked very handsome with his eyes closed.

It struck Delia that it was as if he was lying on a tomb and she gave a little shudder.

She was frightened in case, despite what the Marquis said, he was dead.

Then she told herself that there would be time to attend to him later.

The first thing was to take the men away from the Marquis's property.

Without speaking, the Marquis lifted her into the saddle and then he gave her the reins of his horse to lead him back again.

He then climbed back onto the carriage and drove back quickly to The Hall.

Lucille was where they bad left her in the centre of the drive.

She looked very lovely in her blue dressing gown.

She held the reins in one hand, her pistol in the other.

The two wounded men were still lying where the Marquis had thrown them and Delia could see the blood streaming over one man's wrist.

There was a crimson patch on the coat of the other and they started to expostulate.

The Marquis dragged first one to his feet and then the other.

He thrust them into the back of the carriage.

At first they spoke in Russian, as if unable to express themselves in English, until one man managed to bellow,

"We dying! We need doctor!"

"Then you will have to be clever enough to find one," the Marquis replied.

He slammed the door of the carriage.

Getting onto the driver's seat, he picked up the reins.

The horses, which had obviously been driven a long distance to reach The Hall, were too tired to be obstreperous. And they moved as if resigned to their fate.

The Marquis started back the way they had come.

He drove more quickly than he had when he carried Lord Kenyon and Delia thought that the wounded men would find bumping over the uneven ground extremely painful.

'It is what they deserve,' she moved.

At the same time she did not like to think of anyone, even a Russian, suffering.

The carriage reached the road and Delia handed the Marquis's horse, which she was still leading, over to Lucille.

"I will go home and look after our patient," she said.

As she spoke, she looked at her sister in surprise.

She had now realised for the first time that Lucille was wearing her dressing gown.

But without speaking she turned and rode home and into the stables.

Fortunately neither of the grooms were about at this time of the night to ask questions and she put her horse into his stall and took off his saddle and bridle.

Then she walked quickly back to the house.

Lord Kenyon was just as she had left him and he looked, she thought, like a Crusader.

She dropped onto her knees beside him to find out if he was still alive.

First she touched his forehead and she found that, although his skin was not warm, it did not have the chill of death.

To make quite certain, she pulled aside the rugs.

She slipped her hand inside his nightshirt to feel his heart.

Only as she touched Lord Kenyon's bare skin did she feel shy.

Then she told herself not to be ridiculous.

He was just someone who was injured and required her help. His heart was still beating, although, she thought, rather faintly.

She wondered what the Russians had done to him to render him unconscious.

She imagined that what had happened was that when he was asleep they had entered his room and they had known where to find him from Mrs. Geary's description.

They had hit him on the head.

And they obviously wished to interrogate him.

Therefore they would not have hit him hard enough to kill him or to damage his brain.

Thankfully there was no obvious sign of any wound.

'We must get him upstairs,' she thought, 'and then send for a doctor.'

But she knew that it would be impossible for the doctor not to talk.

She was certain that it would be a tremendous mistake for anyone locally to learn what had happened to Lord Kenyon.

She felt sure that so far no one in Little Bunbury would know of his exploits in India, but Lucille had said that they were talking about him in London.

That meant that sooner or later the story would be repeated and repeated until it reached the village.

'Before that happens, he must be well enough to cope with it,' Delia told herself.

She went upstairs and found, as she had anticipated, that her father and mother's bed was made up.

It was just in case they had people of importance to stay.

There was lace on the edges of the pillowcases and the sheets. The linen smelt of lavender, as her mother had always insisted that lavender bags were kept in the linen cupboard.

This added to the fragrance, Delia thought, which came from the flowers.

She lit the candles by the bed.

In case they were needed, she found some bandages. Her mother always kept these ready for an emergency.

Then she hurried down the stairs.

She hoped that the Marquis and Lucille would not be long.

They arrived about ten minutes later and Lucille came in first.

"How is he?" she asked as she saw Delia kneeling beside Lord Kenyon.

"He is alive," Delia answered, "but I am rather worried about him and I don't know whether it would be wise to send for a doctor."

The sisters were so closely attuned that Lucille knew what she meant.

"We will have to ask Marcus," she replied. "He is putting my horse in the stables so that no one will know where I have been."

"That is sensible," Delia agreed.

It flashed through her mind that the whole village would be scandalised if they knew what had happened and horrified that Lucille had been riding out in her dressing gown.

As if Lucille was aware of what her sister was thinking, she asked,

"Do you want me to go upstairs and change?"

Delia smiled.

"It's too late now."

At that moment the Marquis came into the room.

Just as Lucille had, he asked,

"How is he?"

"He is alive," Delia told him, "but I do think that we must try to get him upstairs as soon as possible."

"Very well."

He picked Lord Kenyon up by the shoulders and the two girls took his legs.

Somehow, although it was difficult, they took him up the back staircase and in to the bedroom that Delia had prepared for him.

Only when he was lying between the sheets did she put her hand once again on his forehead.

"I think," she said, "they must have hit him on the head to render him unconscious and perhaps he ought to be properly examined."

"I have been thinking about that," the Marquis replied, "and, as it is important to keep what has occurred secret, I am going back to The Hall to collect his valet."

He saw Delia look at him in surprise and he explained,

"I was told that he would arrive later this afternoon with my uncle's luggage. Higgins was with him in India, and I think knows all his secrets."

He saw that Delia was still indecisive and added,

"I remember Uncle Kenyon telling me that Higgins had nursed him through malaria and once when he was wounded after a skirmish. I have a feeling that he would be just as effective as any doctor."

"Then please will you fetch him?" Delia asked. "And if you can think of some way of preventing your household from talking, I will make sure that nobody here reveals where he is."

"I will do my best," the Marquis said, "but as you well know, servants chatter like magpies."

Because this was so true, Delia gave a little laugh.

Then, as the Marquis walked towards the door, Lucille followed him and Delia heard them talking together in low voices as they went down the passage.

She knew then that whatever anybody said about him, she liked the Marquis.

She had not expected a young man to be as quick-witted and masterful as he had been.

Lucille came back and said as she came into the room,

"Marcus and I left those Russians on the main road. They will have great difficulty in explaining what happened to anybody who finds them."

Delia was listening as she went on,

"If they should, which is very unlikely, accuse us of shooting them, Marcus is prepared to say that he found them stealing from The Hall and that he shot them in self-defence."

"The whole thing is becoming more and more like a story out of a novel," Delia exclaimed. "I just cannot believe this is all happening."

"Marcus says it was brilliant of you," Lucille said, "to know that the Russians were after Lord Kenyon."

"We have to thank Flo for that," Delia replied. "She was chattering away all the time I was trying to work on the prizes for the Flower Show, but nothing she said really registered in my mind until I woke up from a dream and remembered what you had told me about Lord Kenyon."

"How did you know the Russians were here?"

"Flo said they had been making enquiries about The Hall because they were writing a book and had even asked about the bedrooms."

"And, of course, Mrs. Geary told them."

"Of course she did. You know that she could never resist talking at length about The Hall and showing off to anyone who would listen how knowledgeable she is."

Lucille laughed.

"Well, for once the village gossip has been of some use and thankfully has saved Lord Kenyon's life."

She looked rather anxiously at him where he lay so still.

Then Delia said quickly,

"I am sure that they have just knocked him out because, if they had wanted to interrogate him, they would not have killed him and that is why they were taking him away."

"I cannot believe all this is really happening in Little Bunbury," Lucille stated. "I used to think it was such a 'dead-and-alive' hole where nothing more sensational occurred than the sound of the cuckoo!"

Delia laughed.

"I think we have had enough excitement for one day, at any rate, but I hope that the Marquis will not be long."

"You have to admit that he can be very efficient when necessary," Lucille pointed out proudly.

"As a matter of fact I thought he was splendid," Delia conceded.

She saw the joy in her sister's eyes and thought it rather pathetic.

"I suppose," Lucille said after a moment, "that what you would really like now is a cup of tea, but it would be a mistake to go into the kitchen."

"A great mistake," Delia agreed. "The one thing we must not do is make the servants curious until I have had time to talk to them and tell them that we have an unexpected visitor in the house."

She thought for a moment and continued,

"Perhaps tomorrow we will be able to say that Lord Kenyon is merely an ordinary guest who was taken ill unexpectedly the moment he stepped into the house."

"If we ask Marcus, I am sure he will think of something," Lucille suggested.

She left the bedroom as she spoke and walked to the top of the stairs so that she would know the moment the Marquis returned.

He was back in a little over half an hour.

With him was a thin wiry-looking man who had very obviously been a soldier.

At the same time he had all the attributes and mannerisms of a valet.

"Good evenin', miss," he said to Delia. "His Lordship says that me Master's in trouble again! It don't surprise me. If I takes me eyes orf 'im for a minute 'e's up to somethin'."

The way he spoke was so funny that Delia had to laugh.

Then she said,

"I am in fact rather worried about his Lordship, because he is lying so quiet and still."

Higgins went to his Master's side.

In an experienced manner he put his hand on his head.

"This'll be painful tomorrow," he said. "They 'it 'im with somethin' blunt, I imagine, and knocked him out. There's no wound, only tender as a pigeon's breast it'll be when 'e wakes."

"Is there nothing we can do?" Delia asked.

"Not for the moment," Higgins answered. "We'll just leave 'im to come round natural-like."

Higgins then insisted that everybody should go to bed and leave him in charge.

Delia showed him the dressing room next door where he could sleep.

"I suppose," she said a little hesitatingly, "his Lordship has explained to you that we do not want the staff here, who are old, to have any idea of what has happened?"

"Yes, I have told Higgins," the Marquis said, "and he is used to keeping his mouth shut."

"Had it well drummed into me, my Lord," Higgins said with a grin.

"I am sleeping only a little way down the corridor, if you want anything," Delia said as they left.

"Thanks, miss. I'll soon get me bearings," Higgins replied.

As they stood at the top of the stairs, the Marquis turned to Delia,

"I don't know how to begin to thank you for saving Uncle Kenyon. If it had not been for you, God knows where he would be at this moment."

"Don't even think about it," Delia replied. "It's so frightening. We can talk about it tomorrow, when perhaps he will be able to tell us more about these men than we know already."

"All I can say," the Marquis remarked, "is that I hope they bleed to death, except that then there would be a fuss about it and we might somehow become involved."

"That must not happen," Delia declared quickly.

She was thinking of Lucille's reputation.

"I agree with you," he answered. "All we need to say now is that Uncle Kenyon is staying with you so that he can more easily get to know my future wife!"

He looked Delia straight in the eye as he spoke.

She could not help thinking that he was determined to get his own way and being rather clever about it.

"I think perhaps that is another thing we should talk about tomorrow," she answered quietly.

"I will be back here first thing in the morning," the Marquis promised. "Goodnight, Miss Wintertons and thank you from the bottom of my heart."

He put out his hand.

When Delia put hers in it, he raised it to his lips.

He walked down the stairs and Lucille went with him.

Delia went to her own room and closed her bedroom door.

It seemed impossible that so much had happened in so short a time and, as she began to undress, she found herself thinking two very strange thoughts,

First, that it was exciting that she would be able to talk with Lord Kenyon again.

Secondly, that although she hardly dared admit it, she now thought that the Marquis and Lucille were well suited to each other.

Then almost as if she was crying out at herself, she added,

'But it is impossible for them to be married – quite impossible!'

She knew in her heart that the Shaw family would never admit that Lucille was an acceptable wife for the Marquis.

CHAPTER SIX

Lucille was eating her breakfast when Delia came into the dining room.

"How is our patient?" she asked and Delia smiled.

"Higgins tells me that he has had a fairly comfortable night, but he became restless about two hours ago."

"I expect he will be conscious soon," Lucille suggested, "and then he will be able to tell us if he remembers what happened to him."

Delia thought that this was rather unlikely.

But, of course, she was rather relieved that Lucille was talking naturally about Lord Kenyon.

There seemed to be no ill-feeling between them as there might have been, considering what his purpose in coming to Little Bunbury had been.

She was just pouring out her another cup of coffee when there was the sound of wheels outside in the drive

Her sister looked round and for a moment neither of the girls spoke.

Then Lucille said,

"I have a feeling that is the Marquis."

"So early?" Delia exclaimed.

Lucille was right.

A minute later the Marquis, without being announced, came into the dining room.

Lucille jumped to her feet.

"What has happened? Is anything – wrong?"

"Good morning – "

He was looking at Lucille in a way that made it quite obvious that he wanted to add an endearment.

He had just stopped himself in time.

Then he turned to Delia.

"Good morning, Miss Winterton. I thought I should come and speak to you before I go off to London."

"You are going to London?" Lucille cried. "But – why?"

There was a note of apprehension in her voice and it was as if she felt that he was abandoning her.

"I will tell you what it is all about," he said. "May I sit down?"

He spoke to Delia and she replied rapidly,

"Yes, of course. I am sorry if I appear to have forgotten my manners, but I am still rather bewildered by what occurred last night."

"That is not surprising!"

The Marquis seated himself at the dining room table and Lucille asked,

"Have you had breakfast or would you like some coffee?"

"I have had breakfast," the Marquis answered, "and I want nothing except to talk to you both."

Lucille sat down in the place that she had just vacated and Delia was listening intently as the Marquis began,

"I thought over what I should say to my staff and I have already told them that my uncle and I were out riding last night when he was suddenly taken ill with a bout of malaria."

He smiled before he went on,

"Everybody knows that malaria violently attacks anybody who suffers from it without any warning."

Delia nodded to show that she understood and he continued,

"I was concerned that it would be too far to bring him back to The Hall, so I decided as we were near The Manor, to bring him here and you were kind enough to put him up."

"I think that is a wonderful explanation!" Lucille exclaimed.

"I then went to collect Higgins," the Marquis finished, "and we are hoping that it will not be a bad attack."

"He has had a good night," Delia said in a low voice, "but he has not yet regained consciousness."

"Concussion sometimes takes a long time," the Marquis remarked.

"At least he is alive," Lucille sighed.

"That is what I was thinking," the Marquis agreed, "and it is all due to your sister."

He looked at Delia as he said,

"I am still wondering how I can thank you."

"Please, my Lord, you are making me embarrassed and I am only frightened in case those – ghastly people should – try again."

"I think it unlikely," the Marquis said, "but I intend to take precautions. In the meantime I have told my butler to send you one of the footmen to help carry trays upstairs and I have also asked a kitchenmaid to assist your cook in the kitchen."

Delia stared at him in astonishment.

The way he spoke made her feel as if the Marquis were taking over the house and she no longer had any authority.

Then before she could speak he went on,

"I have also arranged for my Estate Manager's wife, Mrs. Watkins, whom of course you know, to sleep here every night. She will be no trouble and, although she is very busy at home, I believe her presence here is essential."

Delia stiffened.

She was just about to expostulate at what she thought was quite unnecessary interference and then the Marquis added,

"Although my uncle is ill, it is still correct for Lucille and, of course, you, Miss Winterton, to be chaperoned."

Delia drew in her breath and the words that she had been about to say died on her lips.

The Marquis smiled at her as if he knew what she was feeling.

"I have to think of Lucille's reputation," he stated quietly, "and yours."

"You are going to London?" Lucille asked, as if that thought was uppermost in her mind.

"Last night when I went back to fetch Higgins to look after Uncle Kenyon," the Marquis explained, "he told me that he had brought some letters for him down from London."

Lucille was listening wide-eyed as he continued,

"As there was one from the Prime Minister, I opened it to read that the Marquis of Salisbury told Uncle Kenyon that he had just learnt that he was back from India and wished to see him immediately."

"But that is impossible!"

"I agree," the Marquis replied, "but I think it important that I should inform the Prime Minister not only that Uncle Kenyon is incapable of obeying his command but also of what happened last night."

Delia gave a little cry.

"Do you think that is wise?"

"I think that, since we are afraid that there are Russians involved in this other than the two men whom you and Lucille so cleverly disposed of yesterday, the Marquis of Salisbury must be informed as soon as possible."

"I suppose it is necessary," Delia said a little reluctantly.

"The quicker I go, the quicker I shall be back," the Marquis said, rising to his feet. "Look after yourselves and I am confident that there will be no trouble before I return."

He walked towards the door and Lucille ran after him.

Delia did not move.

She felt as if everything that the Marquis had said had stunned her.

The door opened again and he came back.

"There is something I forgot," he said, "and it is to me rather important."

"What is it?" she asked.

"I was thinking that, as Uncle Kenyon is here and it will be obvious to everybody in the village that we are very friendly, it might be a good idea for you to invite me to open the Flower Show."

Delia stared at him in sheer astonishment.

"Open the – Flower Show?" she repeated a little foolishly.

"Lucille tells me it is essential for me to get to know my own people," the Marquis said with a smile, "and it would facilitate matters considerably if I could meet a large number of them all at the same time."

Lucille, who had followed him back into the room, gave a cry of delight.

"That is a splendid idea," she enthused. "Everybody will be thrilled to see you and talk to you. That is what they have been longing to do."

The Marquis did not speak. His eyes were on Delia and after a moment she said,

"We would, of course, be very honoured and I will tell the Vicar this morning."

"It's much more important to tell Mrs. Geary!" Lucille added irrepressibly.

Despite the fact that she was feeling bewildered, Delia laughed.

"I will do that as well," she promised.

"Thank you," the Marquis said quietly. "We will talk about it when I come back."

He left the room for the second time and Delia felt as if her head was whirling and her whole world had turned upside-down.

Could it be true that Lord Kenyon, having been assaulted by Russians, was sleeping upstairs?

And that the Marquis, despite his deplorable reputation, was to open the village Flower Show?

And that he was obviously very much in love with Lucille?

She knew that there were a great number of difficulties still ahead.

For the moment what was imperative was for her to warn the Hansons that there was a kitchenmaid and footman on the way to help them.

She realised that they would be delighted and yet they might feel, as she had, that the house was being taken over by strangers.

It was impossible to eat any more breakfast so Delia went to look for Lucille.

She found her in the gun room cleaning the pistols that they had used last night as well as the one that had belonged to their father.

"Why are you doing that?" she asked.

"Marcus told me that I am to give one of them to Higgins and that one or other of us is always to be in Lord Kenyon's room."

Delia stared at her for a moment.

Then she said,

"Of course, I should have thought of that. We must take it in turns. Higgins has been with him all night so now he must rest."

She paused before she said with a smile,

"I suppose you want to go riding."

"I did think about it," Lucille admitted, "but it will be rather dull without Marcus."

Delia's lips tightened for a moment, but she said nothing.

"I suppose it's no use pretending that I have not been meeting him every morning," Lucille went on, "because I have! And you cannot go on saying how awful he is, because you must admit that he was really marvellous last night."

Delia hesitated and then she replied,

"Yes – he was."

Lucille gave a whoop of joy.

"I was sure that you would like him when you knew him and, dearest, I am sorry that I was so deceitful – but I could not give him up when you told me to."

"I understand," Delia said quietly. "But you do realise that it is not going to be easy for you to marry him?"

The happiness faded from Lucille's eyes.

"I know," she nodded, "with those proud stuck-up relations saying all the time that I trapped him."

"Perhaps things will all come right," Delia suggested, "but I am sure that you must think about it very seriously."

"I think about nothing else," Lucille answered. "I love Marcus and he loves me and that is far more important than a gaggle of disagreeable old Dowagers looking down their long noses!"

Delia did not reply as she could not help thinking that the Shaw family, if they disapproved of Lucille, could make her very unhappy however much the Marquis might try to protect her.

It also greatly annoyed her to think that anyone should consider Lucille not good enough for the Marquis.

He was a young man with a very regrettable reputation. She thought, however, that there was no point in upsetting Lucille.

She therefore picked up the pistol she had used last night and said,

"I will take this up to Higgins and send him to bed, but I had better keep the other one with me."

"You are leaving me defenceless," Lucille complained, "because Papa's pistol is far too heavy."

She picked it up, put it down again, and commented,

"I cannot believe that anyone would want to kidnap me. So I will just trust to luck and my own common sense."

"Perhaps one of the men should go with you," Delia said hastily.

Lucille laughed.

"I was only teasing. The two Russians are, we hope, completely out of the picture and it is unlikely that there are any more lurking in the bushes."

"I sincerely hope not," Delia replied seriously.

Lucille, however, had already left the gun room and Delia could hear her outside running towards the stables.

'Who would ever believe that all this could be happening in Little Bunbury?' she asked herself

Picking up the two revolvers she went up the stairs to find Higgins.

*

Lord Kenyon felt himself coming back to consciousness through a long dark tunnel.

There was, however, a faint light at the end of it.

He tried to move and a sharp pain at the back of his head made him groan.

Then he was aware of somebody beside him and there was the faint scent of violets.

"You are all right," a soft voice began, "and you are quite safe."

The word 'safe' seemed to register in his mind.

He found himself wondering whether he had been wounded and if he was in a British camp.

It was then he remembered the long trek over hard mountainous ground and the cold wind that had seemed to strike through his body.

He was very tired and he wanted to lie down and rest, but he knew that could be dangerous.

Those pursuing him would not be far behind and all that mattered was that he should reach the British lines.

He remembered that the information he had obtained was vital.

If he was killed before he could communicate what he knew, it might result in the death of hundreds if not thousands, of soldiers.

'I have to go on,' he determined.

Yet he felt that it was impossible for his feet to carry him any further.

He tried to move and groaned again.

A refreshing hand was then laid on his forehead and a moment later something damp and cool.

"Go to sleep, you are quite safe and no one shall hurt you."

It was the same musical voice that he had heard before.

Somehow it was reassuring, almost as if his mother was speaking.

Lord Kenyon then felt himself slipping away as if he was carried on a cloud.

*

When Lord Kenyon awoke again, he had the feeling that he had been asleep for a long, long time.

He opened his eyes.

He saw that he was in a room that he had never seen before.

It was not the stony hilltop that had been in his dreams and he lay wondering hazily where he was and why.

Then there was somebody beside him.

This time a young lilting voice that he had never heard before asked,

"Are you awake? Can you hear me?"

Very slowly he looked to where the voice had come from and he thought that he must be dreaming or else he was dead.

He had never imagined that anybody could look more like an angel.

She had fair hair like a halo round her small pointed face.

Huge blue eyes were looking down at him enquiringly.

"Where – am – I?" he stuttered.

"You are quite safe and no one shall hurt you. Would you like something to drink?"

Lucille did not wait for an answer.

She fetched a glass of fresh barley water mixed with lemon juice that Delia had left beside the bed.

Higgins had forbidden her to lift Lord Kenyon's head, so she put her arm around his shoulders.

He could move just enough for the glass to be tipped against his lips.

Even so, she felt him give a wince of pain.

"Soon you will be better," she said. "Now go to sleep."

Lord Kenyon wanted to expostulate that he had no wish to sleep. He wanted to know where he was and why there was an angel giving him a drink.

But it was too much effort.

The pain at the back of his head was too intense for him to think of anything else.

He closed his eyes –

*

When Lord Kenyon woke up again, he could hear Higgins. He thought he would know his voice anywhere, saying,

"E's 'ad a good night, Miss Delia, and sleepin' natural. If you asks me 'e'll soon be 'isself again."

"I do hope so. It is frightening how long he is taking."

"Now don't you fret, miss, and with a guard in the house, we can all take it easy."

"That is what you have to do too, Higgins, so go and get some sleep."

"I don't mind admittin' I could do with a little bit of shut-eye," Higgins agreed.

Lord Kenyon heard the door close and then somebody moved to his bedside.

There was the scent of violets and he knew that he had listened to this voice before.

She stood there quietly beside him and then, as he opened his eyes, she made a small sound that was one of delight.

She must have gone down on her knees and when he could see her, her face was on a level with his.

"Can you hear me?" she asked.

It was difficult to speak, but after a moment he said, "Y-yes."

~145~

Delia made a little sound of pleasure.

"Do you know who you are?"

"Yes – I am – Kenyon – Shaw."

"Then your concussion is over. I am so glad."

She sounded so delighted that he wanted to smile.

After a moment he asked,

"Where – am I?"

"You are at The Manor House, my Lord. You may remember that you came here when you first arrived from London."

"The – Manor!" he said slowly. "Miss – Winterton?"

"That is right."

He thought about this for what seemed a long time before he said,

"I – don't – understand."

"I will tell you all about it when you are better, but there is no hurry."

Lord Kenyon looked into the two grey eyes that were so near to him.

"You were – angry with – me!"

"Yes, I know, but I am not angry with you anymore, only glad, so very glad, that you are better."

"What – happened? Why am I – here?"

"I will tell you all about it soon and it is very exciting, but for now you must go to sleep."

"I am – tired of sleeping."

Now his voice sounded stronger and almost petulant.

Delia gave a little laugh.

"I am not surprised. You have been sleeping for three days and Lucille is already calling you 'Mr. Rip van Winkle'!"

Lord Kenyon's lips twisted into a smile.

"I suppose – you have – some explanation for what – appears to me to be very – strange behaviour?"

"If you will go to sleep now, I promise I will tell you all about it when you wake up."

"I am – not going to – sleep!" Lord Kenyon asserted firmly.

He closed his eyes for a second.

He felt surprisingly a hand moving slowly and rhythmically over his forehead.

It was soothing and very pleasant.

While he thought about it, he slipped away into what his brain knew was a deep healing sleep.

*

The Marquis had not yet come back from London and Lucille and Delia were waiting impatiently to see him.

"Surely he will be here before dinner?" Lucille had speculated a dozen times.

They had finally gone upstairs reluctantly to change.

It was only after a light meal and they had returned to the drawing room that they heard the Marquis arriving.

Lucille did not wait for Hanson or the new footman to open the door and she ran into the hall to open it herself.

"You are back! You are back!" she exclaimed rather unnecessarily.

The Marquis stepped out of his chaise.

"Yes, I am indeed back and I am sorry if I am late," he replied. "But I had a great deal to do."

He lifted her hand to his lips and just for a second they looked into each other's eyes.

Lucille knew that she wanted more than anything else that he should kiss her.

Then to her surprise she realised that the Marquis was not alone. There was a man with him.

The Marquis took her by the hand and drew her into the hall.

Only when they were inside the house did he say,

"May I introduce Captain Ludlow? I will explain everything when we are in the drawing room."

The way he spoke made Lucille realise that it was something very confidential.

She did not comment as the footman in the hall was bringing in a suitcase.

The Marquis walked towards the drawing room taking Lucille by the hand and Captain Ludlow followed.

Delia was waiting for them and the Marquis said,

"Good evening, Miss Winterton, I am sorry I am so late. May I introduce Captain Ludlow, who has come back with me?"

He looked to see that the footman had closed the door behind them before he added,

"Captain Ludlow is here at the request of the Prime Minister to guard my uncle and I can only hope that we are not imposing too much on your hospitality."

His eyes were twinkling as he spoke.

The whole scenario was so unexpected that Delia found herself laughing.

"Nothing will ever surprise me again," she said. "Have you and Captain Ludlow had dinner?"

"Knowing that we were going to be late, we stopped on the way," the Marquis replied, "and actually we have somebody else with us."

"Somebody else?" Lucille enquired.

"Yes," he answered. "The Prime Minister insisted that there should be two specially picked men, Captain Ludlow and Major Dawson, on guard until the Russian who planned the attack on my uncle has been apprehended."

"Do you think that there is somebody else trying to kidnap him as well as the two men we wounded last night?"

The Marquis nodded.

"The Prime Minister is sure of it. Viscount Cross, who as you probably know is the Secretary of State for India, is convinced that the Mastermind behind this outrage would stay out of reach, waiting for my uncle to be brought to him for interrogation."

Delia gave an exclamation of horror and the Marquis said quickly,

"You must not be afraid. Once all three men are behind bars, you will be able, I hope, to forget that anything quite so unpleasant ever happened."

"That is true, Miss Winterton," Captain Ludlow said, speaking for the first time. "The only difficulty for the moment is to apprehend the third man, who will undoubtedly have given the orders."

"And you think he will come here?"

"Not here," Captain Ludlow replied, "but to The Hall."

"Because he will think that Lord Kenyon has been taken back there," Delia said, working it out in her mind.

"Exactly," Captain Ludlow agreed. "But we can hardly leave you unprotected nor, of course, Lord Kenyon."

"How is he?" the Marquis asked.

"I think he is a little better," Delia responded, "and if you and the Captain would like to go upstairs to see him, I will order some refreshment. You are quite certain you want nothing to eat?"

"Nothing, thank you, but I would like to show Captain Ludlow where my uncle is sleeping."

"May I come with you?" Lucille asked.

In answer the Marquis put out his hand.

She slipped her fingers into his.

As they left the room, once again Delia was feeling that her world had turned topsy-turvy.

She was not quite certain how she could cope with it all. She had the feeling, however, that there was no need for her to do anything.

She could just leave it to the Marquis to give the orders.

By the time they came downstairs again a footman had brought in a bottle of her father's excellent claret as Delia thought that it was what they would appreciate after such a long drive.

There was also a bottle of champagne in the ice-cooler.

To her surprise, however, Captain Ludlow refused and said that he would prefer a non-alcoholic drink because he was on duty.

The Marquis poured himself out only a small amount of the claret and Delia thought that he was showing her very obviously that he wished to keep a clear head for anything that might happen.

Now she was sure anyway that his dissolute days were over.

The Marquis did not stay long, but left Captain Ludlow with them.

He drove back to The Hall, where, as he expected, Major Dawson was waiting for him.

A little later Lucille and Delia went up to bed.

They looked in on Lord Kenyon to see if he was still asleep.

"Everything is becoming more and more exciting," Lucille whispered to her sister.

"But still very frightening!" Delia remarked.

"I am sure that these Officers and, of course Marcus, will catch the Russian who was trying to kidnap Lord Kenyon. Then I would hope that everything will return to normal again."

"I pray so," Delia said.

She then remembered that even if Lord Kenyon's personal problems were solved, there would still be Lucille's.

She had not forgotten the reason that he had first come to Little Bunbury.

It was to dispense with the 'common woman' who was trying to trap his nephew. He had even offered, she recalled, to 'pay her off'.

She wondered what he would next do as soon as he recovered and could think clearly again.

*

Two days later Delia sat beside him for several hours.

He had not moved or opened his eyes.

Suddenly she found it impossible to hate him as she had done at first.

And she was vividly conscious, as she sat sewing, how handsome he was.

Now all she could think of were the acute dangers that he had passed through.

She had learnt already a great deal about his exploits in India from Captain Ludlow and even more from the Marquis.

The Prime Minister, he told them, was horrified that the Russians should have followed Lord Kenyon so quickly and they were clearly determined to interrogate him.

"Would they have tortured him?" Delia had asked in a low voice.

"They would have tortured him and then killed him," the Marquis replied.

Delia gave a cry of horror.

"Can these things really happen in England?"

"It happened because Uncle Kenyon has been so brave in India. The Prime Minister told me that the service he has rendered the Government and the Empire is one of outstanding bravery, but it is a tale that can never be told until everybody concerned with it is dead."

"That means, I suppose," Delia had said a little wistfully, "that we shall never know the half of it!"

"That is true," the Marquis agreed, "and I am sure if we try to make Uncle Kenyon talk, he will close up like the proverbial clam."

"Those who know about him and they are very few," Captain Ludlow remarked, "are amazed that any man could have done so much and so cleverly without dying at least a dozen times."

"You are – quite certain he is – safe here?" Delia asked him with a little tremor in her voice.

"The Major and I will do everything we possibly can to ensure it," Captain Ludlow replied quietly.

Delia was aware that now it was Captain Ludlow who slept in Lord Kenyon's bedroom and he was with them only when Higgins was on duty upstairs.

Both Officers were fully armed for any eventuality.

Delia wondered if anybody outside the house had the slightest idea of the tension they were experiencing inside it.

Nothing was more difficult than having to wait for something to happen.

Now she stopped massaging Lord Kenyon's forehead and rose to her feet. She looked down at him and thought that he looked young and vulnerable.

Delia was suddenly afraid that he might have suffered brain damage from the blow he had received.

'Please God,' she pleaded, 'let him get well quickly.'

It was a prayer that came from the depths of her heart.

It did not strike her as strange that she should be so concerned over him.

She walked back to her seat in the window.

Outside she could see through the diamond panes the huge marquee that had been erected in the paddock and she remembered almost as an afterthought that tomorrow was the day of the Flower Show.

Excitement over the news that the Marquis was to open it had run through the village like wildfire.

Mrs. Geary was very voluble on the matter and fortunately no one was curious about what was going on at The Manor.

They were too busy talking about meeting the Marquis for the first time and this swept every other topic of conversation from their lips.

It made Delia want to laugh when she realised that every woman was determined to make herself look smart for him.

Even Flo had said to her when she had come in yesterday morning,

"I suppose, miss, you haven't got a few flowers I could 'ave to trim me bonnet, the one I wants to wear at the Flower Show?"

"Flowers?"

"You know, miss, them silk 'uns you 'as on your gowns. I wants to look me best for 'is Lordship."

"I am sure he will appreciate it," Delia smiled.

She found some pink roses and forget-me-nots that she had put on one side until she and Lucille were out of mourning.

There was only one month of mourning to go, she thought now.

Then Lucille could wear the blue that matched her eyes. Delia was not aware of it but the lilac gowns she wore as half-mourning were a colour that became her almost more than any other.

Her grey eyes were like violets and Lucille had no idea that she looked as beautiful as the flowers whose scent she distilled in the spring.

'The Marquis will be a great success at the Flower Show,' she mused, 'and they will soon forget the stories about him that percolated down from London.'

At the same time it would take longer to erase the impression that he had made with his noisy, vulgar house parties at The Hall.

It was now difficult for her to believe that he was the same man.

Once Lord Kenyon was in danger he had taken charge in what she knew was an extremely impressive manner.

Also, she had to admit, few men would have considered her household difficulties.

He had provided her with not only a kitchenmaid and a footman but also a housemaid and an odd job man.

Jacob came in every day to assist in bringing in the coal for the stove in the kitchen and he carried large jugs of water up and down the stairs for baths.

'If only the Marquis was an ordinary man, I am sure that Lucille would be very happy with him,' she told herself.

She knew only too well how women could make the life of a young woman who they disapproved of an absolute misery and they would continually find fault and whisper insidiously about her.

'Oh – Mama – what can – we do?' she asked in her heart, looking up at her mother's portrait where it hung over the mantelpiece.

It was this same portrait that Lord Kenyon found himself staring at later on in the evening. ,

The sun was sinking and the rooks were going to roost when he opened his eyes.

He was aware for the first time that his brain was becoming clear and he no longer felt as if his head was filled with cotton wool.

Now instead he was able to look around him.

He was aware first that over the mantelpiece there was the portrait of somebody he had seen before.

He was looking at a woman who was very beautiful. She was so beautiful that he felt that the artist must have exaggerated the loveliness of his model.

Then he remembered that he had seen her two grey eyes looking at him in anger.

Beneath the portrait was a glass-fronted case in which there were a number of medals and he found himself recognising them.

He was wondering who they belonged to until he heard somebody come into the room.

It was a woman and she said in a low voice to a man whom he had been unaware of,

"Dinner will be ready in twenty minutes, Captain Ludlow. As I expect you want to change, I will sit with our patient."

As she spoke, Delia walked across the room.

She stood aside so that Captain Ludlow could pass her underneath her mother's portrait.

Lord Kenyon could see quite clearly that Delia was even lovelier, if it was possible, than the portrait.

He waited until he heard the door close behind Captain Ludlow, whoever he might be.

Then, as Delia would have moved towards the window, he said,

"Miss – Winterton."

She started and then came quickly towards him.

"I hope I did not wake you?"

"I am – awake and I feel much more like my – old self," Lord Kenyon replied.

"I am glad, so very glad," she enthused. "We have been very worried about you, but Higgins was quite certain that your concussion would soon be over and then you would be back to normal."

"That is how I am feeling at the moment," Lord Kenyon said, "and I want to know what has been happening and why I am here."

"Do you feel strong enough, my Lord?"

"I am strong enough to be very disagreeable if I cannot be told the truth!"

Delia laughed.

"Very well, but, if you find it boring, you can always slip back into unconsciousness!"

Lord Kenyon put out his hand.

Quite accidentally it found hers and surprisingly his fingers tightened.

"I am listening," he said.

Delia, who had sat down on the edge of the large bed, began her story.

She told him exactly what had happened.

Except that they had no idea as to whether the men had spoken to him or had just crept into his bedroom and struck him while he slept.

Her voice was very quiet and gentle as she carried on with the story.

She spoke of how they had stopped the carriage and found him gagged and bound on the back seat.

Because they were afraid that other Russians might go to look for him at The Hall, he had been brought back here.

And this was where he had been ever since.

Lord Kenyon listened to every word without taking his eyes from Delia's face.

As she finished, he said,

"I am very sorry that you should have been put to all this trouble."

"I am only so thankful that we were in time to prevent you from being spirited away."

"And you and your sister shot the men who were kidnapping me?"

"My father taught us how to shoot when we were young as if we had been boys and we were therefore careful not to kill them, which perhaps was a mistake."

"No, you were absolutely right," Lord Kenyon said, "and so was my nephew in leaving them on the main road to explain about their injuries to whoever was prepared to listen to them."

"The Prime Minister has sent us two guards," Delia told him, "Captain Ludlow, who was in here just now, and a Major Dawson, who is staying at The Hall."

"But nothing has happened so far?"

"Nothing," Delia answered. "And I dislike waiting."

Lord Kenyon smiled.

"I agree that when one is in action it is far easier than being patient."

"Is that what we have to be?"

"I am afraid so. And you know now how grateful I am to you."

Delia was suddenly aware that he was still holding her hand and she moved.

"We will talk about it further when it is all over," she suggested, "but now I will go and find you some dinner. You have not eaten anything for a very long time and I only hope that you are feeling hungry."

"Now I come to think about it, I am," Lord Kenyon replied. "May I add that I am very fortunate to have such a charming hostess?"

She glanced at him as if she thought that he was mocking her.

Then, having rung the bell, she came back to his bedside and he asked her,

"Have you forgiven me?"

She did not pretend to misunderstand what he meant.

She was aware that he was waiting for an answer from her.

And after a moment she said,

"It has been difficult these last few days to think of anything but keeping you alive and wondering when your – enemy will – strike again."

"I knew when Marcus told me who you were," Lord Kenyon said, "that I had made a great mistake and now I can only say that I am deeply sorry."

"I think I – understand," Delia said hesitatingly.

She felt embarrassed by what he was saying.

It was impossible to explain to him that she not only wanted him to live, she also wanted to have the chance of talking to him.

Then the door opened and Lucille peeped in.

"Are you here, Delia?" she asked in a whisper.

Then she realised that her sister was standing near the bed and that Lord Kenyon had his eyes open.

"You are awake!" she exclaimed.

He looked at her and the conversation that they had had came back to his mind.

"I am not in Heaven after all," he remarked.

"So you heard me!

"Yes, I heard you and I also saw you and thought that I must have died and you were one of the angels I had always expected to find in the next world."

"Did you really think that?" Lucille enquired. "I must tell Marcus."

"Tell me what?" Marcus asked from the door. "I could hear you all talking in here and I could hardly believe that it was with Uncle Kenyon."

"Well, it is," Lord Kenyon replied, "and Miss Winterton has been telling me about the excitement you have been having, which I would not have expected in Little Bunbury!"

"That is what we have been saying," Lucille remarked, "but the people here have been told that you are suffering from malaria, so you are going to have to listen to dozens of them giving you descriptions of the fevers they have had and going into great details about their symptoms."

"In that case I shall continue to remain unconscious!" Lord Kenyon exclaimed.

They all laughed and then Delia said,

"I am sure we should not all be in here talking to you and tiring you out. Higgins will be furious with us."

"I have no wish to be mollycoddled any longer," Lord Kenyon said. "What is more, I intend to get up tomorrow!"

"I am sure that is too soon!" Delia protested at once.

"Oh, let him get up," the Marquis proposed. "He can come and hear me make my speech when I open the Flower Show."

Lord Kenyon looked surprised and then he said,

"I can see that you are carrying out your duties as a landowner very seriously."

"I hoped to gain your approval," the Marquis said. "It was Lucille's idea that those who have been curious about me should meet me and I can do it *en masse* rather than singly, which you must admit would be very time-consuming."

The Marquis gave Lucille a look that made Delia think that he suspected an ulterior motive behind what seemed like a sensible idea.

Then Higgins came in, scolding them because there were too many people in his Master's room and telling them as well that their dinner was ready.

"'Is Lordship'll be doin' too much too soon," he grumbled, "and if 'e don't listen to me, 'e'll 'ave a relapse, as sure as eggs is eggs!"

They moved away and only as she reached the door did Delia say,

"I will send his Lordship's dinner up immediately and is he allowed a glass of champagne?"

"Two at least!" Lord Kenyon insisted firmly. "And if anybody tries to interfere, I shall come down and fetch it myself!"

"You shall have everything you want."

Then, with a defiant look at Higgins, she ran after the others, who were already going down the stairs.

"There you are, my Lord!" Higgins said. "That's what comes of 'avin' women givin' orders. They either spoils you or nags you!"

"I certainly find this a very comfortable place in which to be ill!" Lord Kenyon commented.

"That be the truth, my Lord," Higgins agreed, "and nicer people I've never met. There ain't a person in the whole village as 'asn't a good word for Miss Delia."

He did not say anything more, but Lord Kenyon had the uncomfortable idea, although it seemed impossible, that Higgins knew that he and Delia Winterton had battled with each other.

He had unwittingly insulted her the first time he had come to The Manor.

It seemed quite impossible that Higgins could know about it. All the same he was not so sure as servants were always in the know one way or another.

CHAPTER SEVEN

Delia walked into the drawing room and she was thinking as she did so that the house seemed very quiet.

She thought that Lucille could not yet have returned from riding and there was no sign of Captain Ludlow.

She was looking carefully to see that there were no dead flowers in the vases, when Lucille came in through the door.

She was not in riding clothes but was wearing one of her prettiest summer gowns.

"I am sorry to be late, dearest," she began.

Delia looked at her.

"I thought you had gone riding."

"No, I was tired this morning. Marcus is calling for me later and we are going driving."

She spoke quite naturally and without a defiant note in her voice.

Then she asked,

"What has happened to Captain Ludlow? Higgins says he did not come down to breakfast and, when Lord Kenyon woke early, he was not in his room."

Delia looked at her sister in astonishment.

"He left Lord Kenyon unguarded? I don't believe it."

"He must have gone out – or else he has been kidnapped!"

"That is not funny," Delia retorted, "and I could not bear any more disruptions!"

"I am waiting to tell Marcus how good he was yesterday," Lucille said. "Flo says everybody in the village is singing his praises and saying that they had never imagined that he was so handsome or so charming!"

Delia laughed.

"Very different from what they were saying a week or so ago."

"Oh, here he is now," Lucille said excitedly as there was a step outside.

But into the drawing room came not the Marquis but Lord Kenyon.

Both girls stared at him until Delia asked,

"Do you feel all right, my Lord? It has not upset you getting dressed and coming downstairs?"

"I am well," Lord Kenyon replied firmly. "I positively refuse from now on to answer any more questions about my health!"

Lucille laughed.

"You must admit you were very sorry for yourself yesterday."

Having been determined to get up the day before, Lord Kenyon had attempted it and then had a blinding headache.

Higgins, clucking, Delia thought, like a mother hen, had put his Master back to bed.

"I tells 'im what'd 'appen, but 'e wouldn't listen," he muttered. "But, there, that's 'is Lordship. Always 'as to learn everythin' the 'ard way!"

Delia smiled.

But she had been very worried about Lord Kenyon and she was thinking perhaps it was their fault for talking to him for so long on the previous evening.

She was, however, relieved when the Flower Show was over to know that the noise from the garden had not disturbed him and he had slept peacefully all day.

She had gone in to say 'goodnight' to him and found that Captain Ludlow already taking over his duties as 'watchdog.'

She had, therefore, said only a few words to Lord Kenyon and gone to her own room.

She was, in point of fact, feeling really exhausted after all the excitement and clamour of the Flower Show.

An enormous amount of work had fallen on her shoulders. But it was very satisfactory to know that it had been such a success.

She was just about to tell Lord Kenyon effusively what an excellent speech the Marquis had made when there were footsteps outside in the hall.

The drawing room door was flung open dramatically as the Marquis came into the room.

"We have won! We have won!" he almost shouted out triumphantly. "We caught the third man last night and now all three of them are behind bars!"

"What are you talking about? What has happened?" Lucille asked him.

She had reached the Marquis's side.

He put his arm around her as he replied, speaking to Lord Kenyon,

"I can hardly believe that everything went exactly like clockwork, just as Major Dawson had planned."

"Suppose you tell us about it?" Lord Kenyon suggested quietly.

"You know we are all dying with curiosity," Lucille added.

Lord Kenyon sat down in one of the armchairs.

Delia sat in another and the Marquis, still with his arm round Lucille, said,

"Ever since I brought Major Dawson back from London, he and I have slept in the room you occupied at The Hall."

"Surely that was dangerous?" Lucille exclaimed in horror before anyone else could speak.

"Not when you hear what we did," the Marquis replied. "We made a dummy of Uncle Kenyon and put it in the bed, making it appear as if he was asleep. I slept behind a screen and the Major slept on the floor hidden by the curtains."

Delia was listening, her hands clasped together.

It was impossible to believe that the tension of the last days was really over.

"We did not talk about it," the Marquis went on, "for the simple reason that we had nothing to report. Then last night, as Major Dawson expected, a man crept in – "

"And you were waiting for him," Lucille interrupted irrepressibly.

"I had just settled down, expecting another night when nothing happened, when I heard the door creak. I knew at once that somebody was coming into the room."

"It must – have been – frightening!" Lucille murmured.

"He carried a small lantern in his hand," the Marquis continued, "which gave him enough light when he held it up high to see, as he thought, that Uncle Kenyon was fast asleep in the centre of the big bed."

"What did he do?"

"He stabbed him three times with a very sharp dagger before we came from our hiding places."

"H-he – *stabbed* him?" Delia exclaimed in horror.

"There is no doubt," the Marquis said to his uncle, "that he meant to kill you!"

"The Russians don't like being defeated," Lord Kenyon commented slowly. "What happened next?"

"We tied him up," the Marquis answered, "put him in a carriage and came back here to collect Captain Ludlow."

"We none of us heard him leave," Delia remarked.

"Neither did I," Lord Kenyon admitted, "but it is the way they are trained to move around like ghosts and if necessary to be invisible."

"What happened then?"

"Major Dawson and Captain Ludlow interrogated him while they drove me back to The Hall."

"Did he talk?" Lord Kenyon asked in surprise.

"He talked because he knew that he was on a charge of attempted murder, and there was no possibility of his escaping."

"What did he say?"

"He said that he saw you step aboard a ship at Bombay and he recognised you from an incident that had taken place on the North-West Frontier.

Lord Kenyon nodded as if he remembered the incident in question and the Marquis continued,

"He and the two men whom Delia and Lucille wounded also embarked without, and I am sure that this is important, communicating with anybody else as to where they were going or what they were doing."

Listening, Delia knew by the expression in Lord Kenyon's eyes that he appreciated how important it was.

"They travelled Steerage," the Marquis went on, "and followed you first to London and then when you came to The Hall. The man we caught last night, who was the brains behind the whole thing and a very nasty piece of work, knew that this was their opportunity."

"So they kidnapped you!" Lucille exclaimed.

"We were quite right in what we surmised," the Marquis agreed. "They intended to interrogate Uncle Kenyon and find out all they could about the disposition of our Regiments. And then kill him!"

Delia gave a cry of horror.

Lord Kenyon looked at her, but he did not speak, and the Marquis said,

"Instead they will undoubtedly lose their own lives and, as it is a matter of national security, the trial will be held *in camera*."

He smiled as he finished,

"Nobody will ever know what has occurred here or how fortunate Uncle Kenyon is to be alive."

"I am very grateful to you, Marcus," Lord Kenyon smiled, "and I am sure that the Prime Minister and the Secretary of State for India, who will be told what has happened, will want to thank you as well."

He looked towards Delia as he said,

"Of course I must also express my thanks to my hostess, who has suffered a great deal of inconvenience."

Delia made a murmur of protest, but he continued,

"Besides being completely responsible personally for putting one of my assailants out of action."

"Everybody has been splendid!" the Marquis beamed.

"Including yourself," Lord Kenyon added. "And I have heard that your speech was so successful that the whole village is now completely captivated by you."

"I rather enjoyed the sound of my own voice," the Marquis admitted. "In fact I am going to take Lucille's advice and take my seat in the House of Lords."

He looked down at Lucille as he spoke.

The expression on his face was so unmistakably loving that Delia felt that it was almost embarrassing.

Then the Marquis said,

"Lucille and I have an appointment and we will tell you all about it when we come back. In the meantime I am sure that Delia will be glad that you can now move back to The Hall any time you wish without any fear of intruders."

As he spoke, he and Lucille walked towards the door and before Delia could ask them where they were going, they had left.

She found herself alone with Lord Kenyon and felt somehow a little shy.

As if he knew what she was thinking, he said,

"Your sister is putting all the right ideas into my nephew's head and I can only think now that it is a pity they did not meet sooner."

Delia did not reply.

She felt that this was not the right moment to talk to him about Lucille and the future.

Instead she said after a moment,

"I am glad – so very very glad that we need no longer be – afraid of those Russians attacking you."

Lord Kenyon did not reply and she went on,

"Do you think that your nephew was right when he said that the top man did not confide his intentions to anyone before he left India?"

"I am sure that is correct," Lord Kenyon answered. "Every Russian employed in that sort of espionage work is very ambitious to bring off a coup and to establish his own success."

He saw that Delia was listening and he went on,

"I am absolutely convinced from what Marcus said that they boarded the ship in India without indicating to anybody where they were going or what they intended to do."

He looked at her for a moment before he went on,

"If the three of them just disappear, there will be no questions asked and they will soon be forgotten by their own people."

"It seems almost – cruel!" Delia exclaimed.

"The rules of the game are so secret that every man has to act on his own initiative and is, to all intents and purposes, responsible only to himself."

"That is what Papa told me," Delia replied.

She saw Lord Kenyon look at her in surprise and she explained,

"My father was in the Bengal Lancers and he told me in confidence, although I am sure that it will not matter telling you, that just once he took part in *The Great Game*."

"I was very impressed with your father's medals," Lord Kenyon remarked. "I saw them in my bedroom."

"Papa was very proud of them and because he told me so much about India, which he loved, I have longed to have the opportunity of talking to you in depth about that mysterious country."

Lord Kenyon smiled.

"I am ready to answer any questions you want to ask me. But why does it interest you, apart from the fact that your father served in India's most prestigious Regiment?"

"Papa and I used to talk about the country, its customs and religions," Delia answered, "and I found it all so fascinating. I have read a number of books on Buddhism

~173~

and anything I could find in the library about the Palaces and Temples."

There was a yearning in her voice that Lord Kenyon did not miss as she added,

"But that is not the same as seeing them for myself."

Lord Kenyon asked her again,

"Why are you so interested?"

Delia thought for a moment.

Then she said,

"I think perhaps in India there is a spirituality that is not to be found in other countries. I know, of course, that their Sanskrit writings go back to the distant past and so much of what we think of as civilisation came from India."

Her voice died away and after a moment Lord Kenyon said,

"You surprise me. At the same time that is what I might have expected."

She looked at him a little puzzled and he said,

"I knew when I looked into your eyes that you were not just a very beautiful young woman. There is a beauty within you that comes from something deeper and far more fundamental."

Delia smiled.

"I think what you are saying is the most wonderful compliment I could ever be paid. I only wish it was true."

"I think it is true," Lord Kenyon responded, "and that is why I can only say again that I want to answer your questions, if you ask them of me."

Delia parted her lips and bent towards him.

As she did so, the door opened and the footman who had come from The Hall announced,

"The Viscount Cross to see his Lordship."

Both Lord Kenyon and Delia looked up in surprise.

A distinguished-looking man advanced across the room and Delia rose and held out her hand.

"You must forgive me, Miss Winterton," he began, "for calling so early in the morning, but I have a message from the Prime Minister for Lord Kenyon and I am so delighted to see that he is on his feet again."

"It's good to see you," Lord Kenyon replied, holding out his hand.

Delia tactfully moved towards the door, saying as she did so,

"Would your Lordship like a glass of wine or would you prefer a cup of coffee?"

"I would rather have coffee at this early hour, if it is no trouble," the Viscount replied.

Delia smiled and closed the door.

She gave the footman in the hall the order to bring coffee as quickly as possible to the drawing room.

Then she went into her mother's sitting room and she was thinking as she did so how different the house seemed with so much activity going on in it.

She was aware as well how quiet it would be once Lord Kenyon had gone.

With him, of course, would go the excellent servants who had come from The Hall to help out.

Lucille would be spending most of her time with the Marquis with or without her permission.

She would therefore be very much alone.

She tried to tell herself that she would find plenty to do, as she always had in the past.

Yet she knew that if she were honest that this was untrue.

What was more, when Lord Kenyon went back to London she might never see him again.

It was then she knew that she wanted to be with him more than she had ever wanted anything before in her whole life.

She wanted to talk to him and she wanted, if nothing else, to watch him sleep.

She was all too aware of how handsome he was and he was so different from any other man she had ever known or imagined.

Quite unexpectedly she felt her eyes filling with tears.

'I love him!' she confessed to herself. 'But there is nothing – nothing I can do – about it.'

She thought despairingly that her love was hopeless.

Just as her yearning for India was hopeless.

Lord Kenyon had come here to reprove the Marquis for becoming so involved with Lucille.

He would certainly not think of her as being anything but beneath his condescension.

He was polite and grateful, but once he had left The Manor she was quite that certain he would never think of her again.

She felt the tears start to run down her cheeks.

The future was like walking in the darkness without a glimmer of light to give her any hope.

*

A long time later Delia stood at the window looking out with unseeing eyes into the garden full of flowers.

She heard sounds in the hall that told her that the Viscount was leaving and she thought perhaps that she should go out and say 'goodbye' to him.

Then she was aware that her eyelashes were wet and that there were tearstains on her cheeks.

A few minutes later she heard the sound of wheels as the Viscount drove away.

It was then that she knew she could see Lord Kenyon again and be alone with him.

It might be her last opportunity.

It was, therefore, something she must not miss.

She wiped her eyes and then she looked at herself in the small gold-framed mirror that hung on the wall.

She thought that she looked pale, but there was no reason why he should notice that she had been crying.

She opened the door, crossed the hall and went into the drawing room.

Lord Kenyon was standing by the window looking out into the garden.

It was just what she had been doing.

She had the distinct feeling that he too was not seeing the sunshine nor the butterflies hovering over the flowers.

She thought instead that his thoughts were on India, perhaps on the bleak barren rocks on the North-West Frontier.

The dangers that he had encountered there might still menace him.

She reached his side before he realised that she had come into the room.

"Your visitor has gone?" she asked. "I hope he did not bring you bad news."

"No, indeed," Lord Kenyon replied. "He was aware that Marcus and Major Dawson had been extremely brave in capturing a man who, he was told this morning before he left London, had been a considerable menace in India."

"He is of importance then?"

"There is a great deal more to be discovered about him," Lord Kenyon replied, "but he is thought to have been the instigator of a plot that resulted in a large number of our troops losing their lives."

"Which is something he – cannot do any – more," Delia remarked.

She was thinking, as she spoke, of how nearly Lord Kenyon had lost his own life.

As she looked up at him, their eyes met.

And there was an expression in his that she did not understand.

They both stood looking at each other without speaking.

Then the door opened and the Marquis and Lucille came in.

Delia turned round, realising that her sister was wearing her prettiest bonnet and she had bought it for the Lord Lieutenant's garden party.

It seemed to her rather strange that she should be wearing it just to go driving with the Marquis.

The two of them walked hand-in-hand across the room and Delia was aware that they had something important to say.

There was a poignant little silence before the Marquis announced,

"I think, Uncle Kenyon, and you, Delia, should be the first to know that Lucille and I are married!"

Delia gave a little gasp and he went on,

"We could not go on arguing as to whether we should or should not do so and I was completely determined that Lucille should be my wife."

His voice was defiant as he continued,

"I had no intention of waiting until she was out of mourning or for my relatives, whose opinions do not interest me, to have a great deal to say on the subject!"

"You are really – married?" Delia managed to stammer.

"We have just been married in the Chapel at The Hall by the old Vicar."

"Who christened me," Lucille added. "It was a beautiful service and I only wish, Delia, that you could have been there."

"I thought it would be a mistake if you were doubtful and disapproving," the Marquis said simply.

He paused for a moment and, when Delia did not, he speak went on,

"Now, before you start claiming that we have done the wrong thing, Lucille and I are going on our honeymoon!"

"I see you have it all planned!" Lord Kenyon remarked.

The Marquis smiled.

"We are going to Paris to buy Lucille a trousseau, then to Venice and after that I intend to hire a yacht and explore first the Mediterranean and then perhaps the Red Sea."

He looked at his uncle with a challenge in his eyes as he spoke.

Lord Kenyon replied slowly,

"If you come as far as India, I hope you will call on me."

"You are going back to India?" the Marquis enquired.

"Within a few weeks."

"And how shall I find you if we do travel that far?"

"I shall be in Calcutta a great deal of the time."

Lucille had been listening and put her hand on Lord Kenyon's arm.

"You are not angry?" she asked. "In fact I have a feeling that you think we have done the right thing."

"I think Marcus is an extremely lucky young man," Lord Kenyon replied. "He has not only found himself a very beautiful wife but also a very sensible one."

Lucille gave a cry of delight.

And standing on tiptoe, she kissed Lord Kenyon on the cheek.

"I knew you would understand," she said, "but Marcus was afraid that you would be stuffy about it. I promise you that I will make him a very good wife and he is going to be the best Marquis of Shawforde there has ever been!"

"I am quite prepared to believe that," Lord Kenyon agreed, "and besides being reliable in action, I hear he has considerable vocal achievements!"

Lucille laughed and the Marquis said,

"If you are still thinking about past misdeeds with Lucille nagging me I shall have no chance but to reach the very high standards she expects from me."

The Marquis was looking at his uncle.

Lucille was now looking at Delia.

She moved closer to her to say in a very low voice,

"I know you will understand, dearest, when I say that I could not lose him."

"No, of course you could not," Delia replied.

Lucille put her arms round her sister and kissed her.

For a moment they clung together as they had ever since they had been children.

Then Delia asked,

"Are you really leaving now?"

"We are leaving at once," the Marquis said firmly. "We have a long drive ahead of us tomorrow and I want to cross the English Channel tomorrow afternoon."

Lucille laughed.

"He has it all planned out and by the time we come back from our honeymoon, I am sure that I will be like an Eastern wife, walking three paces behind him and agreeing to everything he says!"

"I doubt it," Lord Kenyon remarked. "And if you come to India, you will find that Eastern wives are very bossy in their own homes and indeed you will feel far sorrier for the downtrodden Indian husbands than for their wives!"

"Now, don't put ideas into her head," the Marquis admonished. "I love her just as she is. At the same time I intend to be Master in my own house."

"I will let you," Lucille said, "as long as I can be quite certain that there will be nobody else there but me."

"I think it would be difficult to find anybody as lovely. But one never knows."

He was teasing her, and she pouted at him.

Then he said,

"Come along, we must go. The horses will be getting restless."

Lucille flung her arms around Delia's neck.

"Goodbye, dearest," she said, "the last thing I was deceitful about was to have my boxes already packed! But Marcus is going to buy me wonderful gowns in Paris."

"Take care of yourself," Delia sighed.

"I shall be far too busy taking care of Marcus and preventing him from finding French women enticing to think about myself!" Lucille laughed.

She lifted her face to Lord Kenyon, saying,

"Tell your family I am not as bad as they suspected and I am very very glad that you are alive and well."

"Thank you," Lord Kenyon replied.

He kissed her.

They walked to the front door and there was the chaise and four horses waiting outside.

Lord Kenyon shook the Marquis's hand.

"Goodbye, Marcus. I will support you in every way I can and try to come and see me in India."

"It is something I will greatly look forward to."

Taking Lucille by the hand, he helped her into the chaise.

Picking up the reins he gave the groom just time to jump into the seat behind before they drove off.

Delia watched them until they had left the drive for the road.

With tears in her eyes she walked back into the drawing room without speaking.

She could hardly believe that it had all happened.

Lucille was actually married and was now the Marchioness of Shawforde.

She heard Lord Kenyon come into the drawing room and close the door.

Because she did not wish him to see the tears in her eyes, she stood at the window where she had been standing before.

She heard him come towards her.

As he joined her, she said in a very low voice,

"Please – you will – help them? I know it is – not going to be – easy for Lucille – where your family is concerned."

"I promised I would help them," Lord Kenyon replied, "and I have already thought of something that will convince my relatives better than anything else that Lucille is the right one for Marcus."

"W-what is – that?" Delia asked.

She could not control a little tremor in her voice.

Lucille had looked so radiantly happy and they were both so confident about the future.

She felt that she could not bear it to be spoilt by Lord Kenyon's sisters or by anyone else in the Shaw family.

He did not answer and so she asked after a moment,

"You said you had – something that would – convince them. What is – it?"

"It is that Lucille's sister should be the Vicereine of India!"

What he had said did not seem to make sense and Delia turned her face towards him, saying,

"I-I don't – understand."

"It's quite simple," he said. "I am asking you, my darling, to marry me!"

Delia thought that she must be dreaming.

Then, as she saw the expression in his eyes, she felt his arms go round her.

Her heart turned over in her breast. It began to beat in a strange tumultuous manner that made it impossible to breathe.

Slowly, almost as if he was savouring the moment, Lord Kenyon drew her closer to him.

Then his lips were on hers.

As she felt the pressure of them against the softness of her own, Delia felt that the sunshine dazzled her eyes.

At the same time it invaded her whole body.

She was suddenly transported into a wonderful magical Paradise that she had never dreamt could ever be hers.

The darkness of despair that she had felt because of her love for Lord Kenyon now vanished.

A brilliance of light shimmered round them and yet was part of them both.

His arms tightened.

He kissed her until he took her heart from between her lips and made it his.

She was no longer herself, but a part of him.

This was the love that she had always wanted and thought she would never find, the love that she had believed only a few minutes ago was absolutely hopeless.

"I love – you! *I – love you*!" she wanted to cry out.

Yet there was no need for words.

She realised that the marvellous magical feelings that were sweeping through her were what he was feeling too.

He kissed her until they were both dizzy from the wonder of it.

They were floating in the sky.

"My precious, my beautiful one. How can you make me feel like this?"

She looked up at him and he said,

"I love you, but I never knew that love could be so perfect or so completely invincible and there is no defence against it."

"Do you – want – love?"

"I want you," he asserted. "I knew when I was unconscious that you were beside me. I could smell the scent of violets and when I saw your grey eyes looking into mine, I knew that I could not live without you."

Delia made a little murmur.

"Y-you – might have – died."

"Thanks to you, and you only, I am alive and now you have to go on looking after me and saving me for the rest of our lives."

"That is – what I want to do, but I – thought it was – impossible."

"You love me? Tell me you love me!"

"I love you – so much – that I am – afraid."

"Of me?"

"No – that I shall – wake up to find that – this has all been a – glorious – dream and you – despise me."

"I never did that. I thought when I first saw you that you were unbelievably lovely and I might have known that you were what I have always been looking for and thought I would never find."

"Oh, darling – is that – true?"

"I shall have to convince you and the first thing we must do is to get married."

"Like Lucille and – Marcus?"

"Exactly! They have set an example we must follow."

"Will not your – family be – very shocked?"

"If they are, we shall not be here to listen to them!"

Delia looked at him and then almost as if she read it in his eyes, she asked,

"You are – taking me with – you to India?"

"Do you think I would leave you behind? We have to leave in about three weeks' time. In fact after our honeymoon."

"It will be – thrilling to be in – India with you," Delia murmured. "At the same time – I shall be so desperately – afraid that – something might h-happen to you."

She hesitated over the words.

There was no need to explain what she was feeling.

"All that is over," Lord Kenyon said quietly. "My days on the North-West Frontier are over. As I have just told you, my precious, I am to be the next Viceroy and I shall need you to help me in what will be a difficult but very rewarding task."

Delia understood what he was saying.

She drew in her breath.

"I-I am not – grand – enough."

"As my wife, you will be very grand," Lord Kenyon assured her, "and my family will respect that. Which is why I feel that your fears with regard to Lucille are quite unfounded."

His eyes were twinkling as he added,

"I saw in your father's room this morning a history of the Winterton family. As it is quite a large volume with a long family tree included at the end, I am sure that we shall find some significant connection between your family and my own."

Delia was looking up at him.

He knew she was listening as he went on,

"Anyway, if there is any contention about your blue blood, I will have your Family Tree copied out and sent to them, so that they can digest it at their leisure."

Delia laughed.

"You are making it – all sound amusing – but I am still afraid that they will – resent Lucille."

"In which case she will have her husband to defend her and, as the family will want to be invited to stay at The Hall and be on good terms with Marcus, who is not only the Head of the Family but also an extremely rich man, I am sure you will find that your fears are groundless."

Delia laughed again and said,

"And of course – they will be – very impressed with you."

"So I should hope. To tell you the truth, my lovely one, I am rather impressed with myself!"

"I suppose the – position has been offered to you not only as being the most – suitable person, but also because it is – difficult to reward you in any – other way for all you have done."

"You are being perceptive, my darling, and rather clever."

He pulled her close to him as he added,

"You are not to worry about any of these things, but only concern yourself with me. I want your love and I want it completely and absolutely."

He kissed her lips before he went on,

"I adore everything about you. But I want every beat of your heart, every breath you draw and every thought you think to be about me."

His lips were very close to hers, but he did not kiss her and she knew that he was waiting for an answer.

"That describes – exactly what I am – feeling at the moment," Delia whispered, "but I had no idea that – love was so exciting – so thrilling, and at the same time – so powerful."

Lord Kenyon knew why she said the last words.

"This is what Marcus has found that love is invincible, and I know now that he would have married Lucille wherever she came from or however lowly her origin."

He paused before he went on,

"He and I are incredibly fortunate that we have found the two most beautiful women in the world. And their father commanded a Regiment I admire above all others. And their mother was as beautiful as they are."

"That is the sort of thing I want you to say," Delia cried. "I could not bear it if Lucille and I had – always to be humble and – grateful because you – had lifted us up from what you describe as a 'lowly origin'."

"Instead, my beautiful one, you are on a pedestal," Lord Kenyon replied, "and I am a humble worshipper at your feet."

He kissed the softness of her neck before he added,

"I adore you, I love everything about you and without you my life would be completely empty."

Delia made a little murmur of happiness.

Then, as she put her head against his shoulder, he kissed her hair and said,

"We have only a short time to be alone on our honeymoon and as I am determined to love you, my darling, at every possible moment of it, I want you to send somebody now to fetch the Vicar."

His voice was low and passionate as he added,

"We will arrange to be married first thing in the morning!"

"You feel – well enough to – do so much?" Delia asked quickly.

"I am already planning how to be careful so that I am not too tired to make you realise how much I love you."

There was a touch of fire in his eyes and Delia drew in her breath.

"We will therefore stay tomorrow night and perhaps for two or three more in the Bridal Suite at The Hall."

He paused for a moment before he went on,

"As my brother and your father quarrelled, I think you may not have seen it, at least not since you were a child."

"It – sounds very – exciting."

"It will be, my precious," Lord Kenyon promised.

He drew her closer.

"After that we will go to my house in Somerset, making the journey slowly and carefully."

He saw the joy in Delia's eyes and he said,

"It belonged to my Godmother, who left it to me. She was a very dedicated gardener and I want, my darling, to see you amongst the English flowers."

"You know I love – flowers."

"You are like a flower yourself. In India there is a great deal of beauty, but duty and pomp and pageantry will sometimes make it impossible for us to be alone together every minute of the day, however much I would want it."

"As long as I can – see you and – hear you, I must not be – greedy."

"I want not only to see you and tell you how beautiful you are," he replied, "but also to kiss you, touch you and make sure that you are mine."

"I am yours – completely and – absolutely!"

He looked down at her lips turned towards his, her eyes soft and shining with happiness.

"What has happened," he asked, "to the young woman who hoped that she would never see me again?"

"She had been – taken captive – conquered and is now your – prisoner!"

As his lips touched hers he said,

"I told you that love is invincible and it is no use fighting against it."

Then he was kissing her, kissing her not gently and tenderly, but fiercely, demandingly and passionately.

He was the conqueror, the victor, the man who had achieved everything he desired in life.

Delia was not afraid. She knew that this was the love she had always sought, the love that was strong, demanding, overwhelming and, as he had said, invincible.

She surrendered herself completely to the strength of his arms and the insistence of his lips.

He carried her once again into a Paradise where there was only the music of the spheres, the scent of flowers and the burning heart of the sun.

This was the glory and splendour of love, which comes from God, is God and was to be theirs for all Eternity.

OTHER BOOKS IN THIS SERIES

The Barbara Cartland Eternal Collection is the unique opportunity to collect all five hundred of the timeless beautiful romantic novels written by the world's most celebrated and enduring romantic author.

Named the Eternal Collection because Barbara's inspiring stories of pure love, just the same as love itself, the books will be published on the internet at the rate of four titles per month until all five hundred are available.

The Eternal Collection, classic pure romance available worldwide for all time.

Printed in Great Britain
by Amazon

86251040R10116